The Ancient Manuscript of a Toxic Wizard Family

by daisan the coward

Inquiries and Book Orders should be addressed to:

Great Writers Media
Email: info@greatwritersmedia.com
Phone: (302) 918-5570
16192 Coastal Highway, Lewes DE 19958, USA

ISBN: 978-1-960605-77-1 (sc)
ISBN: 978-1-960605-78-8 (ebk)

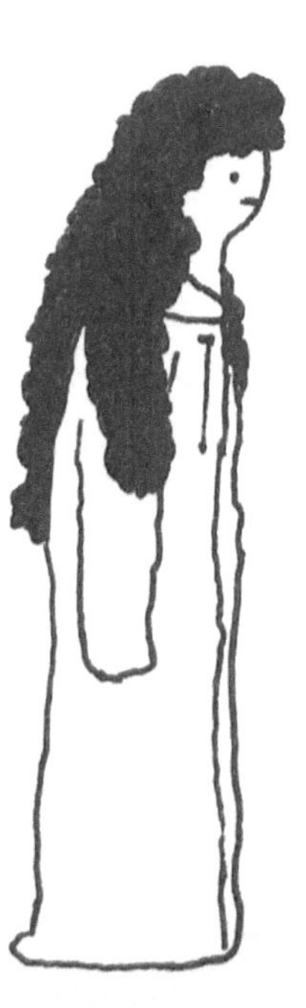
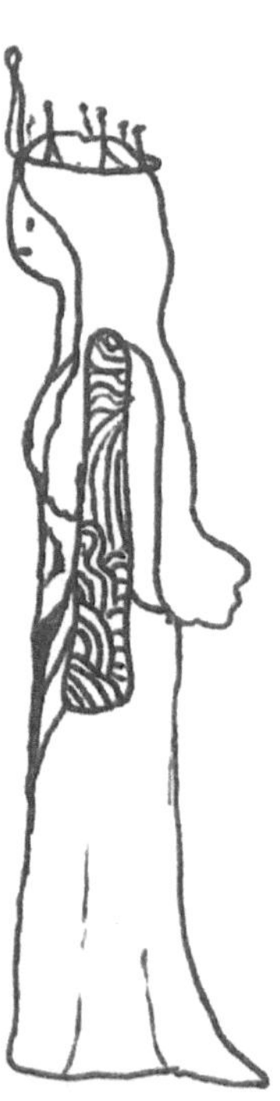

Elijah's Introduction

Every manuscript in this book is historically accurate. They were all written by members of a strange royal family with no last name. They are windows into the shady personal lives of these mysterious figures- taken directly from their own journals, letters, and even a weird gray box that can fit on someone's head. Every story is a secret glimpse into someone's life. Under normal circumstances, this book could be considered a violation of their privacy. However, all of the stories you're about to read happened in another universe to people you will probably never meet anyway.

I'm sorry if I'm confusing you. I will now briefly provide some background before I simply plop you into a pool of rich information.

Shlangovia: perhaps the worst name for something ever conceived. It refuses to roll off the tongue. It feels wrong to say. Nevertheless, it's the official title of an entire civilized world. The landscape consists primarily of rolling hills covered in coniferous forests. The farther north you go, the more mountains there are. The farther south, the more sparse and flat everything becomes. It existed (or exists) in an alternate timeline from whichever one you're currently reading this in. It existed and thrived in a distant reality for thousands of years. It was my opus. Yes. I did create this world. That probably sounds impossible, but eventually it won't be.

You must know that I am writing to you from near the end of time. Specifically, Earth 1-199923, year 3900. This book is from the future. The earth caught on fire if you'll believe it...and no, it's not necessarily my fault. My point is that whatever you think you know about technology and science is microscopic compared to what mankind will discover later.

I doubt you're very curious as to how I (just a normal human) made an honest-to-god, organic world. Too bad. I will divulge anyway. Sometime in the early two thousands, I sent a capsule into a distant earthian reality of the past - before the foundational rocks of earth had even formed. Out of it flew five floating guys. These guys were kind of like gods that I created. Their bodies weren't organic, but their consciousness was downloaded from real people - five of my closest colleagues actually. They were given authority in that realm and I re-organized their memories so they wouldn't get depressed floating around in space for thousands of years. In my opinion, they were the most philosophically and intellectually qualified people for the tasks that I would assign.

They created life. They also brought a fancy camera with them. It sent signals into cosmic pathways leading forward in time. For those of you interested in knowing, you can't send a living organism forward in time, but you *can* send a frequency. So, I had given one of my guys a transuniversal camera. Instead of feeding a live video to me, it would filter through a never ending feedback loop of itself and incrementally blast information into my computer with no clear start or stop. The files were so large and indeterminable, that I had to invent a supercomputer to translate and store all the information. Once everything was filtered through this machine, I could access the video files.

That is how I acquired these manuscripts. I may be the only civilian party to ever access transuniversal information in this way. That's why I'm sharing it. I think these stories are very interesting and should be read.

You see, I'm not a great writer. Even if I was, I wouldn't trust myself to retell these firsthand accounts in my own words. They were written in English, so the documents themselves are direct copies. I don't feel the need to corrupt that.

There is an unlimited collection of stories that I could include in this book, but I want to keep it simple. These manuscripts strictly follow the family lineage produced by Gavin and Angela - two of the most interesting and lovable students I ever had. You might figure out later why I picked those two people specifically (it has to do with Step Eleven).

My main hope is that everyone who reads this book learns something - even if it feels stupid. If you don't learn something, then at least do me the courtesy of allowing yourself to feel something at least once throughout your read. I've been eager to share this knowledge with the public for years. It's been eating me up. Finally, now that the government (or pretty much everything) doesn't really exist, I am at full liberty to shoot this book into the past for generations of people to enjoy. I'm ecstatic. Now, I will share a brief poem.

Shlangovia- you beastly bastard
Serving no particular master

Sigh no more you lovely whore
For you've been freed by disaster

Never after or before
Was there a world so defined by laughter

I love you, harsh and sweet.
My only child, everything.

BLOODLINES

GAVIN
Aife
Boby
Nancy
Bill
Magic Girl
A Librarian
Ryan
Sisters of Sound
Angmen
X X
X
Saorsie
?
Devin
?
?
Amergin
X
= Monarch
X = no offspring
? = ?

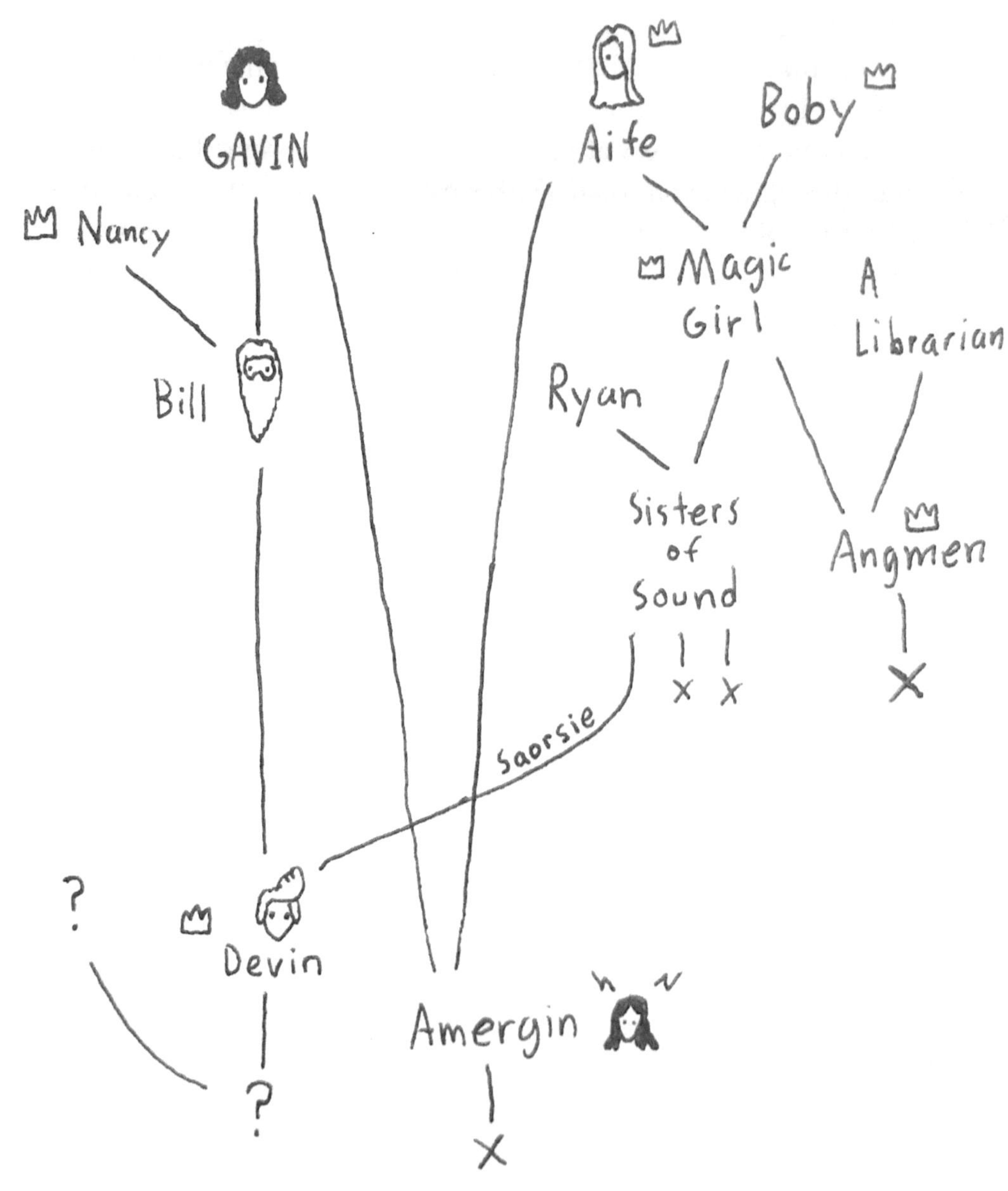

SHLANGOVIA is the only continent on the planet

Gavin and the Mountain People

Chapter One

The gods don't seem to have a lot on their hands, because they check in on me almost every other day. Despite their parental monitoring, I've made it my purpose to complete the task that I was given. They seem perplexed by my drive to do so. I personally find my motivation rather straight-forward. Nonetheless, they discredit my testimony as if it's a cover up for something far greater and sinister. They seem hellbent on prying some kind of incriminating secret out of me. I'm having trouble discerning what they want out of their own existence. I'm going to repeat everything I told them here in this little journal.

I am a man named Gavin. I was sent here probably about two months ago from the distant future of another reality. What is "here?" I don't really know to be honest. Nestled between the foot of a mountain and the oceanside, all I've seen so far is grass and pine trees. It feels like California, but I know it's not. I'm on a different planet. I was told by my teacher that this planet is in its early stages of evolutionary development. Who is this teacher?

Elijah; a mad scientist wizard professor. He shot me through the cosmos in a black, egg shaped pod and burdened me with one task; a task so plain and easy that I should, in theory, find myself living out the rest of my life lackadaisically with a relatively light workload. Basically, I'm supposed to "mess shit up." After the first day, however, I got tired of beating animals to death. Watching the sun set over the ocean becomes a bit of a chore when accompanied by a tinge of anti-environmental guilt. I was forced to reconsider my preconceived notions of problem causing, due to my conscience. I decided to be more- not productive, but proactive with my "messing up" to create more subtle, longer-lasting effects within the ecosystem. I wanted to be efficient with my destruction.

I have been using spells and curses to meddle with certain creatures. For example, I saw a squirrel today. I changed his DNA so that all its offspring will have no fur. There was a duck that came strolling by today and I wanted to see if I could boost its intelligence. After several different incantations it gave me a weird look and sat in my lap. I don't know exactly what I did. I'm not great with biology. I'm more into rocks and shit.

I still haven't figured out why Elijah picked *me* to come here. Perhaps my grades indicated a lack of aptitude for anything much more than failing. The hardest thing to fail at is destruction. It requires no rhyme or reason whatsoever. Frankly, I enjoy it. I would not mind making this my lifelong occupation.

I had my first girlfriend when I was fifteen. All six women after that left me wondering if I was a terrible person. I don't need to ask that question anymore. The gods have kindly informed me that I'm essentially the devil. To them, I'm the master of chaos, the storm king, the principle dark force of the world. Despite this, they really don't seem to dislike me that much. I mean, they allegedly cursed me with immortality, but I'm starting to see a lot of benefits to that. Not that I necessarily want to live forever, but it doesn't sound too bad when setting the existential bullshit aside. I guess I don't have heaven and hell to worry about.

Death is a release. Pain is constant. Life is a cycle of both. I find it all beautiful. That is why I have decided to carry the yoke of the aforementioned three concepts into my workplace. Like my professor, I inflict life, death, and pain on my chosen subjects when

I deem it necessary. I'd imagine the strange celestial beings looking down on me find it quite annoying, but they don't stop me. I admire their appreciation for free will. Then again, sometimes I wonder how powerful they really are, or if they could even harm me if they wanted to. So far, all they've done is talk.

Chapter Two

My tiny mud house was struck by lightning last night while I was fishing. All my belongings were destroyed. There wasn't even a thunderstorm. In fact, there were barely any clouds out. I was pestered, but I remembered my prior remarks involving the gods' power.

Perhaps the attack was warranted. Although, they seemed to act on a whim for entities of such alleged omniscience. I was beginning to wonder if these guys even knew what they were doing- trying to govern the natural order of a whole world and whatnot. They didn't even have a name for anything. All they ever told me about their planet was that the fish were called *fish*. I already knew that, but I almost felt bad. They seemed so excited to know something that I didn't. I think they are confused. They've obviously been reading my journal, so I'd like to clarify that I don't think they're stupid. They are very cool.

I found something very alarming today. I was walking around at the foot of the mountain where I found a tunnel with an oddly perfect circumference. It was probably four feet high and it looked very deep. I tried to go into it, but got scared. As I was crawling deeper into the tunnel I heard distant voices. They sounded human. I was startled, so I ran away.

I'm going back tomorrow. I need to know what or who made those tunnels. I'm going to bring my spear, a makeshift horn for intimidation, and a peace offering or something. If they try to kill me, we'll see if the curse really works. I'm not necessarily scared of death- moresoe the initial shock in seeing whatever horrendous form these creatures may take. I've always wondered what an alien would look like, but that doesn't mean I'm excited.

Aside from that discovery, not much else has been happening lately. I realized that I don't stand a chance at finding a girlfriend any time soon. Then again, I might as well wait until I'm several million years old, having long since broken several bad habits. Oh wait. On the subject of *things,* I did find a dead seal on the beach today. It was fully evolved. That was confusing. I'm wondering how far along this planet is in its biological evolution. I may have shown up a lot later in that process than Elijah told me. It would make sense if that were the case. I'd imagine that universe hopping, time travel technology is difficult to be precise with. No hard feelings for the guy... even if I do get clubbed to death by a group of primal natives due solely to his inability to operate his own time travel equipment properly.

Chapter Three

There's a lot to unpack about my day today, so I'm going to just describe everything that went down as descriptively as possible.

I ate breakfast. Some fish have arms instead of fins and they seem to do alright out of water, which is why I have (up until recently) theorized that they are a missing link. This scientific discovery tasted about as good as it was interesting. After breakfast I assembled what items I required for any potential encounters with the presumed inhabitants of the mountain. I drew a picture of a lamp then departed from my newly constructed mud hut.

I was shaking uncontrollably as I approached the tunnel entrance. What scared me the most was that it wasn't more than a mile away from my place. I creeped over to the opening. With no idea of what else to do, I blew my horn. I had waited till the sun was fully risen so as not to anger anyone who decided to sleep in. This did not console me when I once again heard those thundering bellows from the depths. I took a couple steps back before I consciously decided to take the position of a strong alpha species- tilting my head upwards and puffing out my chest. I wasn't scared (kidding).

Boom bang. There stood before me, a huddle of small, hunched over, bearded, extremely muscular men. I stood completely still as did they. Both parties looked on each with such perplexity. They seemed like people- just smaller with arched backs and bigger hands. I asked in English who they were. One of them said,

"Aaaaahhh."

I thought this was a sigh of relief- maybe he was glad to know

I had high cognitive function. However, I soon learned it was one of the five words that these poor souls knew. Any others were also just straight-tone vowel sounds. They were clothed with wool which caused me to resign nearly every theory I had contrived on the damn place up until that point- weeks of diagrams down the drain. I fully expected anything weird that would come my way at this point. What I didn't expect was the inherent friendly nature of the small people from the cave. They just walked up to me and handed me a rock. I thought it was cute until I flipped it over- then it was hilarious. What I saw was probably the worst depiction of a woman I had ever seen in my life, carved half haphazardly into stone. She was obviously naked and her hair (I imagine) was supposed to be long and glorious. It looked like noodles. I decided to give these guys a brief art class. I'd not technically received my Masters of Fine Arts yet, but I considered myself qualified to instruct these gentlemen on the ways of art.

Twelve small, wide -eyed men sat in a semicircle around me as I drew what I considered to be a very enticing depiction of a nude human female. They must have agreed with me, because as soon as I looked down from my mountain vandalism, they were all either smiling or had tears brimming their eyes. I was beginning to feel proud of myself until one- no, two- no, all of them started to cry. They held each other and groaned while I stood awkwardly with my brush in hand. I thought they would get boners or something, but they just cried.

Emerging from the narrow tunnel came a group of women- equal in number. They were short and stubby, but hot damn were they something. Maybe it was the months I'd spent without seeing a woman's face, but I could have sworn these were prime specimens. They saw me and scowled. Their indifference was inspiring, but I think they were upset that I made their husbands cry. Each one found their respective partner and held him to her chest while they continued to bawl. I started feeling sick, but then everything made sense. One of the fellows approached me and met me with a warm embrace. It was at that moment I realized two things; one: that these guys were huggers- two: that they had probably never seen good art before. I believe it was eliciting a visceral response.

These people were sensitive creatures. They demonstrated no brutish behavior. On the contrary, I found them to be quite polite for having no real vocabulary. I think they knew I was no match for them physically. What if they just viewed me as a deformed creature? Maybe they cried because they felt so sorry for me and my pitiful art. I decided I was going to teach them English. After they knew how to communicate with me, I would teach them basic craftsmanship, fundamentals of mining, smithing etc. I figured I could maybe help advance their race at a much higher rate. I think it will be good. These are people. I don't want to hurt them, or "mess things up" with them. It was today that I started to wonder if this new discovery warranted the abandonment of my initial mission. With these fine folks, it certainly did.

Chapter Four

I'm now one month into my classes. I haven't found more than twenty-four of these little people, so I've closed applications for this little program. They're starting to bug me, though. They don't seem to respect me much. I think they sense that I'm weak. I also think they're mocking me. I'll say a word- any word. They'll start repeating it very loudly while laughing hysterically. They're learning at the rate of a toddler. I suspect they're only doing this because I entertain them. That said, I have made some progress. They're learning the basic names of everything they either hand to me, or I point out. During these two weeks I also found their little flock of sheep. That's where they got their clothes. It's adorable.

I decided that I'd like to found this little society on civility and rules. No hitting or abuse of any kind is permitted. Neither is profanity. It was agreed upon that if they followed my rules, I would teach them language, reading, writing, petrology, mathematics, art, and briefly-physics. Over the course of only one month I got them speaking half-formed sentences. They're so intelligent. I'm very proud of how far they've come. Speaking of come... I don't think they know what sex is. They all seem to have a selected mate, but they have no kids, and I never see them do anything scandalous. I'm a little worried that I'll have to teach them how to do it. One would think they'd have figured it out on their own by now. Oh god. They'll probably cry if they fuck.

I decided to name them all. Of the men there was Jimbo, Bimbo, Limbo, Homie, Dog, Dildo, Fart, Egg, Skinny, Rocky, Emperor

Palpatine, and Adam. The women were Angie, Mangie, Pansi, Ruby, Saturday, Busty, Crusty, Anime, Elsa, Hotty, Mellissa, and Bearded Girl. The names didn't take long to stick. I just told them who they were and they believed me. Soon they were all calling each other by their given names.

A month in, and I still haven't been into their cave. In all honesty, I don't want to go in there. It's probably really dirty, but then again, who knows? They knew how to bathe themselves before I came along, so maybe they keep their rooms tidy, too.

I try not to pick favorites, but Saturday is good at everything. She learns a lot faster than everyone else. If she wasn't with Skinny, I'd have likely developed a weird crush on her by now. The only person I'm having real trouble with is Fart. He thinks he's better than everyone else or something. He's not very strong, smart, attractive, or cool. He very evidently thinks he is all of those in excess. I keep noticing that his wife, Mellissa, is always a little annoyed by it. I worry about him the most, but I see a unique fire in his eyes. He's stubbornly determined to be the best- far more so than anyone else. That's something.

Egg doesn't like me anymore, because I disciplined him. He kept interrupting class, so I took away his paint brush for the day. I'm starting to really make some close friends. I feel happier than I ever felt on future earth. I'm not distracted by technological vices. I have an entire world to explore and learn about with twenty-four new friends to hang out with every day. It's a dream.

Chapter Five

Alright. I've realized that this place isn't just some half-evolved mud ball. Those walking fish are just like that. Everything is a fully fleshed out, earthlike ecosystem. I've seen tons of birds, a herd of yaks, a fox, frogs, chickens that can fly, and an enormous falcon that I'm worried might carry away one of my friends. I still plan on experimenting with genes and altering DNA, but I would prefer not to destroy this place. It's really nice. I don't know why Elijah said to mess it up.

Today marks one year of being sent to this planet. I decided to give it a name: Shlangovia. It's all I could think of. It came to me in a dream, and I had to write it down. I did so several hundred times. I now have just as many small wooden signs with said title inscribed on it. I intend to disperse them all around the world. I will call this place Shlangovia. The provinces will come later. I don't have a satellite view of the map, but I remember Professor Elijah saying that it's quite smaller than the earth we know. Also, it's just one continent if I remember correctly.

For as long as I've been here I've been sober. That's due to my inability to create alcohol. On the other hand, I would hate for my friends to become alcoholics. I couldn't bring myself to be a hypocrite on the matter, so I've resolved to never personally introduce strong drink into this precious land.

My friends are doing well. They've grown a bit; a foot or two each. They're now very close to a fluent level of speaking and have started creating shit. Bimbo and Limbo made a little wall of stone around the cave entrance. It looks quaint. Dog, Homie, and Busty started a rock band. Saturday made the world's first axe and cut down a big tree for everyone to use. Rocky scares me. He recently killed a wolf with his bare hands and now wears the skin as a cloak. Fart and Mellissa are having marital problems, but we're all there to support them. I think we'll start to ease our way into the stone age pretty soon. They still haven't reproduced yet, and I'm kind of stalling for that lesson.

Skinny keeps getting all philosophical on me. One day while we were tilling the garden, he essentially asked me why everyone exists. I said I have no idea. He started laughing. We ate carrots. It was fun. On a different note, none of these people are willing to separate from their partners for more than a day. None of them cheat on each other or anything like that. They're super loyal. I've tried to explain to them what love is, but they can't seem to grasp it. They're not too keen on abstractions at least for now. After a year of fostering a small society I felt very satisfied with the work I'd done.

Chapter Six

The gods paid me a visit this morning. They started off by ripping me apart emotionally. They made fun of my physical appearance and my small dick. Then they got more serious. According to them I had been tampering with the natural selection process. The small, hairy people were supposed to stay in the cave for much longer and only come out when they had grown much larger. I guess I drew them out prematurely. According to the spirits, I had caused them to become weak and gullible. This actually did make sense. I didn't know any of this stuff was relevant until they brought some things to light.

"It's a lot bigger than you think. They aren't the only people here, and not everyone will be as accommodating to their ignorant willfulness as you are. We made them to be the strongest people in the world. They're intended to reign over everyone else, because they're so well tempered and naturally inclined to be good people. This is why we only made twenty four of them. Each couple can only bear one child over the course of their lifetimes."

I had considered the possibility of other people groups or "races" being out there, but it did not strike me that these mighty, powerful people could be taken advantage of by others. They are inhumanly strong and they're far from stupid. This rebuttal didn't hold up.

"You foolish imp. These mighty creatures have known no hardship or strain. You have neutered them. They're passive, unaware of danger, and *artistic*. They're supposed to be thunderous, stoic, dangerous, and vigilant! You have snaked your way into their ranks and caused them to be weak."

"What is so dangerous about the world? Rocky killed a giant wolf with his bare hands. He broke the damn thing's jaw, then stomped its head in. They're all like that. I don't see the problem here," I said.

"Humans," one of the spirits thundered.

"What?" I shouted.

"Oh shit. We forgot to tell you; we created humans for you. They're very similar to the ones on earth- just a tad dumber. They're not entirely as smart," explained another cosmic voice.

"So you made new people for me to hang out with instead of these people? And these new people are hard wired to enslave and hurt the people I was already hanging out with? So you all got together and decided that I needed new friends? Not only that, but that these new friends would be toxic?" I asked.

"That's an interesting way to put it," one of them laughed. Then they all started laughing. "Well, they're people. People have free will. You are the only earthian human on this planet and that is why you have not suffered yet. That's part of your curse, you know- suffering. We don't really want them to be your friends. They're supposed to hate you. We would've made them regardless of your mistakes anyway. We just want more people. The punishment is more of a perk."

"Then what do you want me to do?" I asked them. At this point I was feeling very small. "It's up to you. You've already done the damage. These corrupted people will be too trusting to outlast any conflict with humans. We don't have any advice, but thank you for fucking up our world."

Silence fell like a sheet on the meadow in which I stood. I was now sweating trying to tell myself that this wasn't truly my fault. Because it wasn't. There was no rule or recommendation about not making friends with people, but apparently doing so was to indirectly commit genocide. I love these people with all my heart, and I've never met someone on earth who I found to be as beautiful. I want nothing to do with the new humans. They sound terrible.

After my sad little meeting I went to the mountain. My friends hadn't seen me like this yet, so they were scared for me. I didn't know what to say, so I just cried while they all huddled around me in a giant group hug. I tried to do some lessons, but they fell apart. I think I'm depressed now. I feel something very dark inside. I feel like the universe is trying to prank me. The most fatalistic, sick, sadistic joke of the cosmos seems to have taken up residency on my back. Now the universe laughs everywhere I walk.

I'm going to try to sleep now, but I'm a little worried that I won't be able to. Maybe my house will burst into flames. Maybe my soul will be sucked out of me the second I close my eyes. Maybe I'll just wake up tomorrow and be content with the natural repercussions of my unbeknownst idiocy. Perhaps I'll feel better after my dreams bring me a fuller understanding of life. I'm not philosophical, but I feel like there are a lot more ways to view this all, morally, than what I may be able to conceive right now.

Chapter Seven

It's been three days since I learned that all the work I've done is destined to be the demise of innocent people. Unfortunately, it would seem that I'm successfully meeting the expectation of my mentor. I believe it is because of this that another space egg landed here today. I was sure to find that Elijah would punish me with some kind of lethal gas, a rabid raccoon, or maybe a child. Instead, he only sent supplies, food, a handcrafted Scottish claymore, and a poem on a small sheet of notebook paper. I was very upset and started to wish I'd never come here. The poem went as follows:

Great wind sways the giant
He has made a false alliance
With the dream of living out his days
Unharmed by his loving ways.

May the might of the sea befall him,
The shaking of the earth swallow him,
The fire of the sky scorch him-
And yet may he stand again.

Blessed and Cursed in one fell swoop.
Gavin is a lucky poop.
All the money to ever mount
Could never buy what he has found.

Life and Suffering hurt his eyes,
But all will soon feel just fine.
Gavin is a tender soul,
Despite his efforts to control.

As you could imagine this poem had a profound impact on me. There's a good chance that this mission Elijah sent me on had a deeper meaning than I originally thought. I've read many of his poems. They are almost always very hurtful, dark, and humorous (which I like). This stylistic deviation has to mean something about how he sees me.

However, I was curious about the claymore. It was beautiful. Upon close examination, I realized that it had inscribed: *The Bleeding Heart of Shlangovia.* Then I began to consider the worthlessness of everything I just described. I am wretched. I looked at the sword then back at the poem again and again. Slowly, a terrible thought began to fester. All twenty four of my small companions are tough, smart, wise, generally quiet, and level headed- all except one; Fart. I knew it from the start. He was slightly lacking in nearly every area of quality an individual can possess. This never meant much to me, but I realized that if his sperm was removed from the future gene pool of these people they would have no weak links. I realized that there was one sure way to ensure the survival of the mountain people.

I love Fart with all my heart. I picked no favorites among my friends. I had to spend two hours sweating and hyperventilating in my tiny house while it seemed to get smaller. This was the last thing I wanted to do. Nevertheless, I'd already made myself responsible for the well being of these people and now their future was compromised. There was one sure way to break that ignorant trust of everything and crush their oblivious softness. I hate it. I hate myself and I will never forgive myself for this sin.

I approached the tent of Fart and Mellisa and stood several feet from the doorway. I called out to them and they crawled into the overcast daylight. Mellissa said something about my face being white. Fart and I locked eyes. Not long after my cheeks were split by rivers of sadness, so were his.

"I love you very much, Fart," I whispered.

"I love you too?" he said hesitantly. Before he could ask me what I was doing I lunged forward and thrust my blade into his heart. He fell and I drew my sword out of his rib cage.

Mellissa seemed to experience every human emotion imaginable within the microsecond that I made eye contact with her. Her breathing increased rapidly and wailing she yelled,

"What the fuck, Gavin?" She couldn't say much more as she crouched down and held her dead husband in her arms. I commited the first murder.

"Gavin!" Roared Rocky several tents away. He was visibly shaking-more terrified than I'd ever seen him. Everyone came out to see what happened and I stood there with a bloody sword. I had absolutely nothing to say. I just grunted and sighed and paced around. Everyone was crying and shouting curses I had told them to never say. I didn't run away, because I hoped someone would kill me, or at least try.

They all gathered about ten feet away from me and were asking me why I did it. I said nothing still. I looked at the ground. I just stood there and looked at the ground. They were afraid to approach me, because I still gripped the sword tightly. Homie emerged with a fire in his eyes and landed a blow on my jaw. He punched me so hard, I flew back several yards. Naturally, this rendered me unconscious.

When I woke up I was uncertain how long I'd been asleep and my face felt wrong. I looked around to see the tents were all abandoned. I stood up and walked around their camp to find everything of value gone. Then I saw the entrance to the mountain tunnel. It was sealed. Somehow they had caused it to cave in on itself. They left me. I realized my jaw was unhinged and probably irreparably broken. I felt around it. Soon it started to crack and pop until it was fully back where it needed to be. I think it had to do with the immortality curse, because I didn't fix it myself.

Chapter Eight

My heart is ripped open. I don't feel at home in my house anymore. I find no semblance of peace when I lay my head down. I'm filled with nightmares. I genuinely can't remember how many days I've now spent alone. I've tried thrice to kill myself, but each time my body healed itself. I haven't eaten anything. I've barely slept. I decided to climb the mountain today and see if I can reach the highest point. Then I would jump off.

I trudged on and on up the steep rocks. Whenever I fell, I just climbed back up to that point again. Two days or so went by while I climbed. There was no cathartic reason for this. Despite said lack thereof, I did move with the speed and drive of someone with great purpose. I just felt the inexplicable urge to do something intense and violent to myself.

When I reached the top of the mountain I saw above the clouds. The still, grayness of everything was now surpassed by an ocean of blue air. The sun was beginning to set. Without my permission, a memory began to play out in my head like a movie scene.

I was cutting down a tree with Jimbo, Bimbo, Elsa, Anime, Emperor Palpatine, and Fart. I thought about the way they looked at me while they asked questions about the world. They saw someone worth looking up to. Regardless of my self-perceived value, they saw someone who they could trust and learn from. I remember trying to explain what parents were to them. They had no reference point, so they started calling me *dad*. I asked them to stop, but they danced around me and chanted it to get on my nerves. My eyes were starting to get misty and they stopped to apologize. I told them I wasn't sad crying. I just loved them so damn much.

I froze in the air while I descended from the mountain top. I probably broke every bone in my body on my way down. It was so fast. Tumbling- an avalanche of loosely bound flesh eventually rolled to a stop on the opposite side of the mountain that it climbed up.

As I lied there paralyzed in a forest of evergreens, I made a decision. I will travel the world. I will walk until my feet fall off. I will fulfill the foretold curse and be a nomad in the beautiful lands. I will find no rest until the end of time. I will leave no discernable trace of myself wherever I go, and I will touch nobody. I will leave the animals alone. I will let the trees grow. I will walk- eating nothing until my body can no longer sustain itself. I deserve more than death. I deserve eternal wrath. I deserve the flames of hell. My suffering should surpass that of anyone to ever live. I have forfeited my right to make new friends. I will be alone forever.

The Angelic Wizard Queen and the Devil

(A Manuscript by Boby)

My name is Boby. I'm three years old, but I am physically and mentally twenty five. That's because my tribe and I were created by the gods to be the very first humans on our planet. We were born out of a marsh. How did I become such a good writer? Well, I was taught by a majestic woman named Aife. She is so smart and good at language and reading and writing. Most importantly, she is good at teaching. Everyone in our tribe learned how to speak from her. She became my wife, because we are in love. This is the story of the devil who tried to tear away my love.

My friend Rowan was watching his sheep when he spotted a deformed man walking around in the marsh. He was so thin he looked like a skeleton. His clothes were dirty and torn. Rowan was worried about him, so he brought him into the village and laid him on the table in his house. Aife and I came over to look at the man. Rowan was rambling on and on about how worried he was, because the man looked like he should probably be dead. The man didn't say a word the whole time. He looked surprised and scared.

We fed him a lot of food and water until he couldn't eat anymore. After he was done, he slept for almost a whole day. When he woke, he was brought into Aife's house. He sat on his knees and looked up at her with confusion in his eyes. We asked him a bunch of questions (even though he didn't answer them). Then, he said his first words.

"Angela?" he said with a stupid voice.

"Who?" she said.

"Angela, what is this?" asked the stupid, skinny man.

"What's what? Who's Angela?" my beautiful wife asked. I'd like to note that my her name is definitely not Angela.

"What the *fuck*, Angela?" he said even more stupidly.

"You need to speak clearly. Where are you from?" she asked. He just stared at her trying to think of something stupid to say.

"You know where I'm from," he said.

"No, I don't," she said.

"Yes you do," he said.

"*No*, Gavin. I don't," she said.

Bird Land

"See! She knows my name, guys! We know each other! We're from the future and she's trying to trick you," the weak man shouted while looking at all the council members circled around him.

"The gods told me what your name is, idiot," my wife said.

"Ok. I won't argue with you, Angela-"

"My name is Aife!" she yelled. The whole room became still. She sighed.

"What a terrible circumstance. This poor man has been living alone, no food, no shelter, nobody to love, all alone- a lonely, lonely man. He has come to my village with his mental ailments, and all I do is shout. What kind of queen am I to treat this feeble creature with such cruelty? I intend to make it up to you, small man. Tonight we are having a feast. We will kill two lambs and we've already killed a white leopard. We will make a cloak for you out of its fur to hide your shriveled limbs," Aife said. The council all applauded the humility of the queen.

"You're a bad woman," Gavin said. It looked like he was starting to cry like a pussy. Aife stood up from her dark, wooden throne and gave him a hug. Everybody else clapped, but I wish she wouldn't have touched him.

That night while I was having sex with Aife she seemed distracted, so I stopped and asked her what the hell was wrong.

"I don't know, Boby. I don't feel good." I knew this was code language for something, but I didn't know what. I asked why she didn't feel good.

"That guy... Gavin. He is evil. I think he has brought a darkness here. I knew him in a past life. We were enemies. We waged many wars against each other."

Gavin. That son of a bitch. He was making my wife scared and uncomfortable- even while she was making love to me. I asked if we should banish him from the village, but she said that was not a good idea. He "needed help." Apparently, even if someone is evil, helping them can make them better. That's bullshit if you ask me, but I did not argue.

After about two weeks of Gavin staying in our village, he

had started filling everyone's heads with terrible thoughts about "psychology." We all know that doesn't exist, but somehow he convinced some of the weaker-minded people of its power. He also started to become friends with Rowan. I didn't have a problem with Rowan making friends, but Gavin of all people? The only reason I didn't stop it was because, really, I was Rowan's only friend. Maybe he could use one more. I told Aife about all Gavin's lies. She dismissed everything. This is when I started to smell fish. My own wife? The wisest woman of all? Buying into the deceit of a crazy, homeless imp? It didn't make any sense.

I realized that my wife would not tell me the truth, and I needed to ask the man how he knew her, or something. I wasn't going to go so easy on him. One thing I've never agreed with Aife on: peace isn't always the only way.

Later that night, I snuck into Gavin's tent, put my dagger up to his throat, and said, "Come with me. I don't want to hurt you. I just want to talk." He must have thought he

was dreaming, because he wasn't scared at all.

I brought him over to the creek. We sat down on a log and I asked him,

"What is up with you and my wife? Part of me thinks you two weren't really enemies." The disrespectful prick started laughing.

"Oh, man. I'm sorry," he said.

"For what?"

"I know you don't want to hear this, but we dated in college." I didn't know what college or dating was, so I asked him what they meant. I was shocked to find out.

"We had sex. We were in love- possibly," he said. I had never felt my heart drop so low in all my life. I hate to admit it, but I started to feel some tears coming on.

"You're lying. She's too beautiful for you!" I cried (admittedly a little too loud).

"That's what I thought too. Apparently she disagrees," he said with a putrid smirk.

"I know what you're trying to do. You want to divide us. You want to cause strife in our town and make us all turn against each other," I said.

"No, man. I'm sorry. She really did date me. Why would I try to divide you guys? You all seem very happy. Rowan told me you and Aife have a lot of loud sex. I think that's cool." Gavin's snaky words started slithering around in my brain.

"Don't tell me about Rowan. You poison his mind. You scare my wife, you now tell me that you slept with her, and you steal my best friend!" I yelled.

"Oh fuck. I didn't mean to do any of that. I am cursed, you know."

"I could tell you were cursed from the moment I saw your eyes," I said. "Well my eyes aren't part of it, so that's just a coincidence." "BOBY!" I heard my wife yelling in the distance.

"Oh dear. Hey man, I'm glad we got to talk. You're doing good. Treat her right," said Gavin as he started to walk away.

"Your tricks won't work on me. You can't manipulate someone who's married to a wizard," I said. He stopped dead in his tracks.

"She's a wizard?" he asked.

"Uh. Yeah. She's the most powerful person in the world."

"Okay, okay, but can she die?" he asked.

"Of course not. She was blessed with eternal life by the gods." "Oh my fucking god!" he yelled.

"Be quiet! She probably heard that! Also please stop using the F word," I asked politely. I was trying to control my temper.

"You have no idea how weird and awesome this is, man," he said.

Just then, Aife and two village men appeared right above us on the edge of the creek wall.

"What's going on, Gavin? Boby, did he hurt you?" she asked. I was in trouble.

"No. We were just talking," I said.

"About what?" she asked.

"You're immortal too?!" Gavin yelled. He just couldn't control himself.

"Wait. No. Shit. This isn't right. Why are- Gavin..." then, for the first time, I saw my wife bawling. Gavin was trying to tell her it was a good thing. Me and the other guys were very confused as to the nature of their relationship. I do believe this uncertainty is what put me off the most.

I didn't understand what I was feeling at that moment, but I knew what I wanted to do. I wanted to punch his dumb face so hard it broke. I wanted to kill him then go to bed with my wife whose judgement seemed very clouded by this liar.

"Aife! He lied to me! He was saying that you went to college and dated each other!" I yelled. Now, I too was getting loud.

"Why would you feed him such lies?" she asked Gavin. It was dark so I couldn't see his embarrassed face, but he apologized just about as pathetically as possible.

"I'm sorry, Boby. My bad. We indeed used to be enemies. That's the truth." I was relieved to hear both of them confirm what I suspected. This man was a little slimy worm.

"Now, Gavin," Aife said.

"I'm warning you. If you continue to infest our homes with deceit and malice, I will be forced to banish you."

"I want him gone tonight," I said.

"We give him one more chance, Boby. Can you do that?" I didn't want to miss having sex that night, so I agreed.

"You guys are so damn nice. I can't thank you enough for letting me stay here," Gavin said.

"Stop cussing. It's not allowed here," Aife said.

"Ok, *Aife,*" he said sarcastically. I didn't get to have sex anyway. Even though this gross little man was clearly a liar, I couldn't shake the feeling that my wife had some feelings for him. She was kissing me less, hugging me more, and having way less sex. This seemed very bad. I still didn't know if he was really immortal. I couldn't sleep that night.

The next day I watched Gavin visit the people and walk around all happy. He was an imposter- a demon wearing a man's skin. His blood ran cold and I could tell. He was a creature from the depths of the earth camouflaging himself as an innocent out-of-towner. He tricked my wife.

Suddenly my eyes locked on him and I was walking straight towards him. He was talking to our butcher. Without thinking for one second, I grabbed the butcher's knife and stuck it deep into Gavin's temple. He fell to the ground, dead.

I wasn't sure if what I'd just done actually happened, but before I could consider my actions, I heard the worst sound I've ever heard in my life. My wife screamed from three houses down and sprinted over to Gavin. It was so loud and terrible that it probably scared me more than the idea of murdering someone.

Blood was running down his ragged clothes and my wife knelt down beside him. She didn't even look at me. She took him into her arms then grabbed the knife. She pulled it right out of his skull. More blood gushed out. I had no idea how to feel about this. I just stood still and watched. Sadness deeper than I've ever felt started to settle around me.

The whole town had gathered around us in a circle. The butcher had backed up into his doorway. Nobody said a word. I had just committed the first murder.

But then- the blood stopped streaming. Gavin's skull and skin pulled itself all back together. His eyes opened and he took a deep breath. He truly was immortal. My sadness left for a brief moment, but it returned when I saw Aife wrap her arms around the resurrected rodent. Their embrace was lasting a little too long for my taste, so I walked over to them and pushed them apart. There were still no words until the idiot finally spoke again.

"Woah. What a curse," he said with blood all over his face and an annoying little laugh. "It's a good curse," my wife said. Then she looked at me. I looked at her with fear and

anger. I felt her slipping away. Then, out of the blue, she proved that she was still wise. "Gavin, I need you to leave."

"What? Your husband just tried to kill me! He-" she stopped him.

"Gavin. *I* need *you* to leave," she said again. There was a long pause. The people around us seemed to be upset to hear this. I was disappointed in how they'd allowed themselves to be enticed by this man's false virtue.

"If you insist..." he said. Then, he really crossed the line. He quickly kissed her on the cheek. I spared no time in kicking his balls. She was mad at both of us, but more at him. The true quality of a man comes when he admits that he is wrong. Unlike me, he did not apologize. He laid on the ground like a baby and chuckled.

By that afternoon, he was gone. Our people didn't need him. Our lives were rich and full because of our queen- *my* queen. It took a couple months for her to start acting normal again. I think his darkness lingered in her soul for that long. Thankfully I caught him- that predator-that rotten, scheming rat. Thankfully I got rid of him before he did something even worse.

As time went on I told the people he talked to about his lies. They were shocked. At first, some of them didn't even believe me. Over time the people realized that whatever was trying to tear our village apart couldn't have been human.

He only looked human. Inside he was a demon- shriveled and thin. He was the devil. This story passed on through my children and hopefully it will be taught to my grandchildren and all my descendants as well. Mankind learned a valuable lesson from Gavin: some men are too good to be true.

Gnomes and Goblins

My First Act of Treachery

This is the first time I've journalled since I was sent to this world. The only thing that really matters is that I've also found some kind of weed to smoke since that entry. I wish I could say that's the only thing prompting this sudden desire to expel my mental vomit. However, I'm compelled to write by something slightly more interesting... and bad.

For over a decade, I was the queen of all humans. I ruled with an olive branch in one hand and my husband's dick in the other. I alone am responsible for the overall education and advancements made by the human race on this planet thus far. They're a real society. So, you're probably perplexed. If I'm still alive, then why am I no longer queen? Well, I'm not alive, at least as far as any human is concerned... but to gnomes I am very much alive. You see, I made a grave mistake. I got pregnant.

Shortly after I bore my first child, I was astounded at how little I wanted to care for her. Boby and I named her Magic Girl, because she was born with obvious powers. At three weeks old she was causing small plants to sprout in the house. Boby was thrilled to have a child; especially a magical one. I, for one, felt like shit. I loved my daughter, but I really did not want to raise her... let alone do so alongside my bumbling ballsack of a husband. In fact, I had grown extremely fucking tired of Boby. I'm still not convinced that he doesn't live solely for his own sexual fulfillment. The good thing about this lifestyle is that it happens to work well for kings. Boby was first in line for the crown. Now he had an heir, so our dynasty would continue. Everything was fine for everyone except me. That's why I faked my death.

There was something ineffable to my indifference. No matter how hard I tried, whenever I looked at Magic Girl, I could not feel any major sense of maternal affection. It wasn't that nothing kicked in necessarily. It felt more like the wrong thing kicked in. I think it was postnatal depression, but I'm not a psychologist. Basically, I knew I needed to get as far away from that life as possible. I wasn't worried about Magic Girl's safety or if she would grow up scarred. I figured one of Boby's whores would love to care for her. She would be none the wiser. She was only three.

I pulled a Joseph on myself. I tore my dress and spilled a rabbit's blood over it right outside the city walls. It was a nice dress, but a worthy sacrifice in order for me to fulfill my plan. I found a beautiful red elk and rode him through the plains for many days. I finally reached a massive redwood forest. The trees soared above me. Very soon upon entering their cavernous shade, I found myself surrounded by the smallest people I've ever seen.

I was a little frightened, because they appeared to be quite feral. This theory solidified when they swarmed my elk and bit his legs. I'm very glad I didn't name him, because his eyes started bleeding and he collapsed on the forest floor. These tiny fuckers had venomous bites. As I stood above this small army and a giant dead elk, I wondered if my "eternal life" was resistant to this vampiric defense mechanism. In my darkest hour, the last thing I expected was for one of them to bark at me in fluent English with an American accent.

"Do you know who we are, bitch?" a very fat one asked.

"No," I said, taken aback by his evident lack of class.

"We're dangerous. We kill giants like you," another one said. Now I was even more curious.

"Wait. You guys have met other giants?" I asked.

"Yeah. He tried to make us his slaves. That's all you evil shitheads do," they shouted. "What the hell are you doing in our woods?" the very fat one asked. For whatever reason, right then, I decided to open up to the strange little people.

"Well, if you'll believe it, I'm running away from the other giants. They tried to make me their slave too," I said. All the munchkins were leaning in, cautious, but curious. They begged me to continue.

"I realized that all they wanted me for was my labour. I worked and worked, but it was never enough. When I stopped working, they punished me. They only liked me for my physical body. I had to escape them. They only like power. They could care less if I'm happy."

"Damn," I heard faintly in the distance.

"That's almost exactly what happened to us," someone said. I asked that they elaborate.

The very fat one took the liberty of enlightening me. He seemed like the ringleader.

"We were lonely forest babies. Full grown, but we didn't know anything. Then one day, a giant came along. He taught us how to talk and build things like houses and tools and how to hunt and farm. Before too long he started making all these rules. When we asked him what the rules were for, he said 'for order.' That's when we realized that order is just another word for tyranny. He was trying to rule our lives. Guess what he said! He said we couldn't cuss or smoke. He pretended to love us, but he really just wanted to use us as his servants. Well, that fucker got something very different from that!" he yelled. His companions laughed and cheered in agreement. I implored him to go on.

Mountain
Person
(full grown
Human
Goblin
Gnome

"One night, we all lifted up his bed and carried him out of his house. We took him all the way to the river. Right as we were about to dump him into it, he woke up and yelled 'stop!' but it was too late. He fell into the current and was swept away! No more Gavin! Stupid fucker." With those final remarks, the crowd once again went wild.

It all made sense now. He was trying to copy me. I found it reasonable to assume that his motivation in raising an army of his own was to impress me or to make me jealous. At best, I found this grand gesture to be sad. I'm not a monkey, so using mimicry as a flirting device doesn't impress me all that much. I almost feel sorry for him.

I looked across the sea of hairy heads amongst the trees. They were all just staring at me. They were peaceful, organized, and collected. I realized that these small ladies and gentlemen did not need a supreme leader to tell them what to do. However, it appeared to me that they could use a wizard friend.

"I've met this Gavin. He's the lord of darkness, king of evil, and founder of mischief. Everything he touches, he destroys. I'm surprised that you were all strong enough to overthrow him!" I said.

Since that moment, I've become close friends with those little guys. They're very smart and ingenuitive. They look like gnomes, so that's what I've been calling them. When they can't reach something, I'm their hero. When I get lonely, they're like my therapists. Gnomes rarely leave the woods, so I just hang out in the forest all day. I've been living with them for several weeks now, and I've enjoyed every second of it.

My Second Act of Treachery

I don't even know how it happened. I woke up this morning and realized that I am effectively the queen of these gnomes. I've only been with them for a couple months, but they worship me. I'm afraid. They genuinely think I'm a goddess. Which- I kind of am? Everything is just happening so fast and it all feels wrong. I am not built to be in charge of shit. For ten years I tried to convince myself otherwise. Now I'm stuck again. Fuck me.

They serve me like slaves, but I avoid all governmental rhetoric. I feel bad, because at this point I'm fairly certain they would die for me. They love my magic. I might try to teach them some spells. I feel bad, because I genuinely see them as my friends. Yet, because of my biological disposition, they seem to innately view me as superior. I think they're deeply wounded by whatever Gavin said. I wouldn't want him to be the father of children, let alone the chief distributor of knowledge to an entire group of people. That's dangerous.

The gnomes had no idea that Gavin was immortal and they genuinely believed he drowned in the river. One night, we caught a young goblin spying on us. I had never seen one before this. His skin was pale white and he had to be about two feet taller than your average gnome. The people of Shlangovia are just small. Even the humans are a bit shorter than the ones on earth. Do I miss earth? Nope, but I'll spare that rant for later. For now, let's talk about the goblin.

Dead giveaway the second he opened his mouth- Gavin got to him. The poor guy spoke with that damn American accent. Gavin and I hold in our hands the responsibility of civilization. I don't really care what Elijah thought - neither of us are qualified for such a thing. I don't know shit about economics, how to lead, or how to protect people. I have no idea what Gavin believes politically, but I worry for his ethics. Obviously he means well in the grand scheme of things, but that never saved someone from being terrible at their job. I had the sneaking suspicion that he was brainwashing an entire group of people to his isolated line of thinking. I really needed to talk with this annoying son of a bitch.

"Who's your king?" I asked the goblin. He was tied to a tree and the moonlight glossed over his little bald head.

"My name is Reggie," he said politely.

"Oh. Sorry. That's not what I was asking," I said.

"I won't tell you anything, ma'am," Reggie said. By now there were probably two hundred gnomes gathered around trying to get a glimpse of this weirdo.

"Now, Reggie, you know that if you don't tell me where you live, or who you're working for, I'll have to torture you?" The gnomes generally seemed to like this idea. Reggie did not, but he was clearly willing to yield his body as a sacrifice for his king. I decided to whisper something to him.

"I know you're Gavin's slave and I need to talk with him. Take me to him. I'll come alone with nobody but you. I won't torture you or hurt anyone. I just need to talk. Please." I made sure my gnomes didn't hear this. To be honest, they did not need to know that their first major accomplishment as a race was a complete failure.

"Ma'am, I am no slave!" said Reggie, escalating the volume of our conversation.

"You don't even know what that is, do you?" I asked. Reggie looked at the ground clearly embarrassed. I decided to change tactics.

"You know what, Reggie? I think you're cool. You've been so well behaved and I like the way you speak. You're a respectful young man. Who here thinks Reggie is awesome?" I yelled to my people. They reluctantly agreed that he was.

"You don't know me. You're manipulating me," Reggie said more softly than anything else he'd uttered.

"I know, but Reggie, I do mean it. I think it would be fun for me and you to hang out for a little road trip," I said.

"Well, it wouldn't really be a road trip. I don't live very far from here," he said.

"So would you like to take me there?" I asked as kindly as humanly possible.

The next morning we saddled up the mini-horse and made our way to Reggie's abode. We walked through the forest, into a meadow, over a creek, through more trees, and finally to the base of a cliff. We then stood between semi-circled trees and a towering crescent wall. There were no houses or caves in sight. That was the first time I was ever tricked by a goblin. It has a negative effect on one's self esteem.

At the top of the cliff was a row of goblins holding large rocks above their heads- ready to drop at any moment. Emerging from the trees were more of them sporting sharpened sticks. I was terrified.

For all I knew, they were going to eat me. Then I remembered that I had powers. Oh right! Angela, you're a fucking wizard who is also immortal. I put a bear spell on them. A bear spell makes someone's brain temporarily view you the same way it would emotionally perceive a bear from only three feet away. It basically just forces its subject to be mortified. They all sort of froze or started doing awkward shit with their hands.

I'd only used this spell once before. There was this girl in college who probably couldn't emotionally handle the concept of not talking about demons for more than one hour. One day, she was trying to convince me that she had met a dead girl's spirit over the phone. Keep in mind, this was while we were doing a lab. I was trying to focus, and she was coming dangerously close to fucking with my 4.0. The value of education seemingly lost on her, I felt that she was deserving of my little punishment. It did not have the desired effect. Our project on the table was smashed by her crawling over it to get to me. The main difference, upon my second use of this spell, was that it didn't cause the goblins any sexual arousal. That bitch was a nightmare, but I was curious to see if I could give an entire army of goblins a hard-on. I digress.

While the pale little guys were shrinking back, a giant stone which rested on the cliffside abruptly disintegrated. The dust collected at the base of the now opened entrance to a cavern. Then, regardless of how I wanted to feel about it, Gavin emerged. Dressed in the same leopard robe I gave him a decade ago, he entered the sunlight covering his eyes with his sleeve. He walked towards me like a panther walks to a river. Why did I write that? I stood there and realized how much I wouldn't mind him fucking me up the ass. He stopped roughly six feet away from me. I wanted to reach out and touch him. Part of me wanted to be a part of him. I successfully withheld the tears that I wanted to shed.

"What the fuck, Angela?" he said. Then I remembered that I was presently terrorizing his little army. I promptly lifted the spell with a faint "sorry." He was visibly angry and confused. I couldn't tell which sentiment was more prominent, but what he said next indicated that there were more than two emotions present.

"What took you so long?" he asked.

"I had a kid," I said. Gavin threw his head back in laughter, followed by his expansive crew doing the same. I wasn't sure if this was appropriate, but that didn't stop me from also laughing.

"You're too ugly to have a kid!" Reggie yelled. Everyone's laughter awkwardly ceased.

"Shut up, Tom," Gavin said.

"Who's Tom? I'm Reggie!" Reggie said; seeming to be hurt by his master's faulty memory.

"Dude! No you're not! Reggie's downstairs," said one of the goblins near the trees.

"Tom, we don't need to use our code names anymore," Gavin said.

"Why not?" Reggie/Tom asked. There was an untimely jolt in momentum as I watched this strange paternal tension build.

"Well shit. Would you *like* to switch names with Reggie?" Gavin asked the young goblin.

"I don't know," Tom/Reggie said.

"Let's talk about it later, ok?"

"Ok," agreed the little guy, while he eyed the grass below him.

"Who's Angela?" I asked in an attempt to shift the mood.

"Oh right. Sorry, Your Highness," Gavin said. His comrades were clearly perplexed by the situation. In fact, I think everyone was perplexed by something or other. He continued.

"Oh god... Ok boys, this is Aife! She's the Wizard Queen of Shlangovia. We will respect her and give her whatever she wants, alright? Tonight we'll put a little feast together. She can stay for as long as she wants and I want you all to be nice to her."

"Uh... Gavin? I've been going by *Apple* lately. Aife is dead. I also can't stay. I just-" I started stuttering only for him to interrupt me.

"Why not?"

"I got more kingdom stuff... you know those gnomes?" I asked. He disregarded this explanation and yelled to his friends.

"Okay guys, her actual name is Apple and she's..." his voice lowered.

"What are you now?" he asked.

"I'm like... a forest person helper friend type of thing. I don't know," I said.

"She's a powerhouse of a woman! And she's awesome and she's also very cool, so don't be mean to her," he yelled.

"Gavin, please shut up," I calmly requested. He was being very obnoxious. He stopped talking, but I could hear the goblins whispering to each other. To my relief, Gavin turned to me and continued in the two-way method of conversation.

"I already know what you've been doing. I've been spying on you. Up until just now, we've been under the assumption that you were a prisoner of the gnomes. I guess that's not the case since you're here now,"

"What?" I exclaimed. The indecisively named goblin decided to elaborate in Gavin's stead. It was cute that he let him. This goblin was clearly very young.

"They were keeping you in a tiny stick house and making you do all their work. Every time we watched, you were either in your little jail, making food for them, or building their houses."

I blushed. Now I was looking at the ground.

"That's really sweet, Aife," Gavin said.

"No it's not!" the what's-his-face goblin shouted.

"She's a nice lady who was getting taken advantage of!" he shouted again.

"Tom- Reggie, she's clearly not a prisoner," Gavin said.

"Well, no, but she's helpless! She's so kind and weak!" the goblin said as he waved his hands through the air.

"I- I- maybe- buddy- we don't-" Gavin was starting to crack. He was getting nervous. "Can we just have a private meeting?" I asked. By then everyone was already walking towards the cave entrance. There was clearly no need to spear me to death.

"Yeah. Yeah, that's ok," Gavin said with a smile.

I was brought into their giant home. I was standing in the largest cavern I had ever seen. Sunlight washed through an opening in the ceiling. Hundreds of feet down was a sort of lake. Along the walls were connected tunnels, one of which we had just come out of. There didn't seem to be that many residents for the space they were occupying. We climbed down a shaky ladder and into a small room. It was clearly where Gavin had made his bachelor's abode. I would come to find out later that he alone carved out these vast subterranean cathedrals. He had gotten very good at magic. He beckoned for his guards to leave, lit a torch, and sealed the door to his proportionately tiny bedroom.

Our meeting lasted for what felt like a day. We touched on too many subjects for me to remember. It became abundantly clear that I was less in tune with myself than I had thought. Our conversations led me to realize that I had been harboring residual feelings for both my old world and its only remnant I now had (Gavin). We disagreed on a lot of large scale philosophical matters, but came to the mutual agreement that we wouldn't fuck with each other's kingdoms unless one of them began to pose a serious threat to the safety of the world.

After making this deal with the devil, I decided to go home. Gavin was on to something. He was hiding underground whilst ruling the goblins. I was now running away from humans too. At this point, both him and I were intent on becoming nothing but myth to our kind. I don't know how he felt about humans, but I realized he's the only one I really like. I don't even like my own daughter. He's the only thing that felt real- not physically. We only talked. There was nothing more than platonic interaction going on in that room (to my slight disappointment).

I remember we talked about how earth didn't have very many plants and we were now engulfed in them. Earth didn't have the same innocence as this place- this baby world. For some fucked up reason, Gavin and I are its parents. Whether we like it or not, we kind of got roped into raising it. I also hate the name Shlangovia, but everyone already calls it that. I was hoping to come up with something cool, but he beat me to the name.

I'm going to bed. In the morning I will make breakfast for some gnomes then build a little house.

Songs of Lord Devin

These are the great songs and epics written for and about the wizard master, lord of snakes, and philanthropist, Devin. They were written by his traveling companion and most loyal friend, Alvin. In the year of 460 Alvin and Devin met at a trading convention in the city of Tire, in a province ruled by Ironland. Devin was impressed by Alvin's beautiful ability to sing. He paid Alvin to write and perform a song about him in the market. According to the great wizard, the song was the most accurate, artistic, profound piece of music he had ever heard.

No man can compare in strength or wit
To the one who has invented it

No blade could he fall by in the land
And the women fall into his hands

No trick or scheme will be a rivalry
For his intellect is -

What am I doing? I don't even want to write this song out. It doesn't matter anymore.

Devin's been killed. I think I would rather write a biography. Yes. That's what I'll do.

As the authors of biographical accounts often are, I am inclined to write a story that embellishes the accomplishments and virtues of His Majesty. However, after deep consideration for those who have suffered because of him, I am compelled to let their voices perorate in this record. I am Alvin the goblin minstrel. I was Devin's closest friend for many years until he died at the ripe age of three hundred and fifty-five.

I am writing this as a parting gift to the world. My time to die has grown steadily closer, and my fear is that I leave the future generations to speculate on who this great king was. I don't want people to think of him as a bad man. I also don't want people to think he was some amazing hero. Though a wizard, he was just as fallible as anyone. I will do my best to report the broadest of truths in equal balance. My aim is not to offend his allies or his enemies. I will not allow my personal opinions on his actions to snake their way into this record. I will tell the story as it is.

ALVIN the MINSTREL

I met Devin when I was fifteen. He was probably about two hundred and ninety or so, but, as all wizards do, he had the appearance of a twenty-five year old. We instantly connected. Neither of us ever found out why. We were nothing alike in any way. Regardless, I left my family's farm to travel with him and study the world. At this time, he was the most wealthy person in Shlangovia. The means by which he acquired his earnings I know little of, and never sought to learn. He was a shrewd businessman and a proficient womanizer. Because of his status and power, he could go to bed with almost anyone he wanted. Consent usually wasn't an issue. Everybody wanted him. In fact, many women and men who had engaged with Devin would live the rest of their lives in a vacuum of emptiness- having already reached the peak of human ecstasy- knowing they will never return there again. After having sex with Devin, everything else feels gray. He could do things to someone's body that normal people just couldn't do.

We rode in a lavishly decorated buggy through the cities where he would conduct his various business ventures. One strange town after the next would gladly host us. Devin was known for his ability to economically stimulate a town in just one day. This was most often done through philanthropy, but sometimes it was accomplished with bribery or blackmailing greedy lords. I would usually excuse his moral errencies in favor of the indulgent lifestyle we lived. Only once did I ever directly question the man (more on that later).

For many years Devin and I engaged in stimulating conversation while I embraced the given position of personal assistant. He seemed entirely against the idea of ever being a king, though it was in his blood. His mother, Saorsie, also rejected her royal inheritance in favor of a musician's lifestyle. This was likely in part, due to her mother's emotionally abusive parenting techniques.

Devin's father, Bill, was a sad wizard scholar and philosopher who moped about in libraries all day and travelled the land- never taking the time to be a real father to Devin. Bill's mother Nancy was the first ruler of Ironland until she was overthrown and murdered by a group of rioters. In Devin's mind, a position of such power would be too stressful and dangerous to maintain. He preferred the lifestyle of a nomad, alleviating the target that would otherwise be on his back.

What set Devin apart from any other wizard was that he was descended from not one, but two magic bloodlines. His mother, Saorsie, was the daughter of Magic Girl and the granddaughter of Aife. On his father's side was Nancy who gave birth to Bill. Nancy was an unpopular ruler. According to rumors, she conceived Bill through the King of the Underworld himself. The combination of Bill and Saorsie's genes proved highly potent. Devin would grow up to probably be the most powerful wizard ever.

Devin shagged so many people during his lifetime that the amount of offspring he may have is immeasurable. Once he shagged someone, he would leave them the next day. He would shag at least one person every day. He would go for almost anyone, too. He was the first human to impregnate a goblin. He didn't enjoy it very much, but he did it more than once. Several men followed in his footsteps. Nine months after his first sexual encounter with a goblin, everyone realized why nobody ever did that. The child that was born grew to be taller and thinner than a human with even paler skin than us goblins. It was too late now, and many others were born. Devin alone may be responsible for the birth of those abominable goblin/human hybrids. Nowadays, they live far south in the desert and cover their faces because they're so ugly.

One rainy night Gavin seemed to suddenly change his mind about royalty. He had just returned from a long walk through the woods for some reason. We were sitting on a log in the forest by a snuffed-out campfire. I asked him why, after all these years, he suddenly felt such a calling. Naturally, he avoided the question. Instead, he showed me a castle he had designed on some paper. It was not a large castle. A deep trench surrounded the walls and the gates were short. He told me that his power as a wizard was unmatched, so the likelihood of being overthrown was very small. He wanted a kingdom specifically for rich people. The general idea was to create a living space and party house for the wealthiest merchants, lords, and ladies. It was to be called "The House of Devin." I told him it was a bad idea. A lot of people would probably want to conquer such a place. In response to my warning he set his hand on a giant tree that promptly turned to dust. There was no reason to debate. He made up his mind.

Not too long after this decision, we found ourselves in a newly constructed castle surrounded by a council of very wealthy people. It wasn't a year after that Devin had instituted what he called a futile system. Apparently, the name stems from the peasant's innate inability to move up in life. Below the castle, nestled in a vast expanse of trees, lied a huge town full of what I believe were technically slaves. To my discomfort, I could order them to do whatever I wanted. I never did such a thing, so they generally liked me.

Like everything else he did, Devin's futile system was founded on lies...kind of. He formulated an entire religion that enticed people to move into his kingdom. His ragers were funded by his subject's taxes. His laws weren't strict, and generally, everyone had plenty of liberty, so he was fairly well-received by his people as far as I know. They didn't even recognize the exploitation taking place right below their noses. Even if they did, however, they probably wouldn't have made a fuss.

The only requirements to be a member of "The House of Devin" were high taxes and conversion to Snakeism. He never felt that an army would be necessary for defense, because he was really powerful. Royalty from afar often visited just to behold his magnificence or maybe see him do a magic trick. Many people regarded that kingdom as a free, beautiful place. The royals got to party, read books, and engage in all sorts of extravagant activities, while the peasants worked and sometimes entertained themselves with small things like drawing. However, there was a special treat that everyone would get once a month.

On every third Friday, Devin would put on a large-scale play. It always involved a male protagonist's struggle for purpose and a giant snake somehow helping him find it. Even after I secretly deconverted from Snakeism, I still enjoyed those plays. They were fast-paced and colorful. Devin would often make use of fire, water, animals, and clever special effects in his productions. It was a grand spectacle reserved only for his subjects.

Devin assigned me the roles of Chief Poet and Minstrel of the kingdom. Before any songs or poems could be written or performed by his subjects, I had to approve of them. If they seemed to discredit Snakeism at all (even indirectly), then I was to outlaw them.

I'm sure you'd like to know what Snakism really was. Well, I will now enlighten you. Many people know that it once existed, but few care to read up on what it was. Unbeknownst to most, Snakeism was revelationally prompted. Allegedly, Devin had a violent encounter with a god.

Once, he was climbing a mountain trying to find the meaning of life. As he reached the top of the mountain, a thunderstorm began to brew. Lightning was flashing all around him and the thunder made his ears ring. He cried out into the dark, angry sky begging for someone or something to show itself to him. The wind and rain only battered him further. He was beginning to feel tormented by a higher power. He tells me that his whole life he had been in pursuit of this strange force that seemed to lead him there.

In desperation he stretched his arms above his head and began harnessing the lightning to his will. It struck his hands without burning them and was sent back up into the sky. He thought that eventually his powers would relent, but somehow the lightning he was redirecting only increased in potency. He sent the beams far beyond the roof of the clouds and into space. He shouted against the thunder with all the fury he had suppressed throughout the course of his life. He cursed the earth and demanded a sign. Large rocks shattered all around him and the mountain on which he stood was shaking viciously.

Then, descending from the heavens was what appeared to be a giant man falling to the earth. Devin moved out of the way. The large, robed entity fell face first into the mountain. The storm suddenly subsided. The moon poked through and the wind ceased. He walked to the slain giant and beheld its size. To his recollection, it was probably fifty feet tall- sprawled out, dead on top of the mountain. He had killed a god.

Devin began inspecting the body at the feet and made his way to the head. The shoes were red. Beneath the glistening white and pink robe was a skin-tight gray suit. The creature had no hair and its skin was gray like a goblin's, but it was far more coarse and unpleasant to the touch. When he approached the head, he saw that it had been split open. Inside of the skull there were no brains or blood. All he saw were tiny flashes of light and hundreds of dead "lightning snakes." The face of the god was burnt to a crisp and unrecognizable, because it had been struck by Devin's lightning.

Devin was overwhelmed with fear and exhaustion. He stood up and froze as a voice from the sky echoed through the mountains.

"Devin, you have killed our friend. You stupid idiot. Why have you done this?" it thundered.

"I apologize, Master of the Universe! I did not intend to hurt anyone. I only wanted to know the meaning of life," he said.

"Oh. I see. You shouldn't use your powers like that. If you ever exert that much energy again, we'll kill you. Now, travel the earth and tell others what you have learned," the voice said.

Snakeism is founded on the belief that the gods are powered by snakes, and that they have a purpose for every individual who will seek them out. Devin believed that snakes were the highest form of intelligent life in the universe, but were unable to do anything because of their lack of appendages. He taught that if you follow a snake for long enough, it may lead you to your destiny. Ever since then, he shared this story with people and convinced them to give him money for his kingdom.

To my knowledge, Devin never had a true lover. To him, sleeping with someone was almost a professional courtesy. He was known to willfully disperse his seed into anyone or anything that he could. Due to this habit, his many offspring would inevitably become estranged from him. Over the course of our relationship, I began to notice that he would only share his deepest thoughts and secrets with me- nobody else. Furthermore, he was determined to provide me with literally anything that I could ever want. I rarely asked him for anything much more than basic necessities. Eventually I wondered if he saw me as a sort of son. I would've made a good son. I was compliant, quiet, and usually of good cheer.

Our unspoken bond lasted sixty-five years. By the time I was sixty, I had been appointed head advisor, governor of two towns, and royal ambassador. Around this time, one of my primary duties was actually to seek out wealthy merchants, royals, and lords to invite to Devin's parties. If you were ever invited to one of his parties one of two things would happen to you. You would either come and have the most fun of your entire life, or you would come and be executed for an offense against the king. If you didn't feel like coming, he would have you killed anyway. You had to show up.

One day I was at a royal feast in the capital of Greenland Two, and I accidentally invited Devin's half uncle to a party. The great King Angmen of the east. Devin never spoke of an uncle, but Angmen spoke very highly of him. King Angmen ruled every city on the east coast of Shlangovia along with several districts by the Fish River. He was known for his brutality in battle. Though he was in fact, a wizard, he actively chose to never use his powers. He was a master at every weapon in the world and never hesitated to demonstrate his prowess to those who opposed him. How did I unintentionally invite one of the most powerful men in the world to a private party? Well, the conversation went a little like this.

"So, do you ever have parties here?" I asked.

"Oh, yes! Quite often, actually," Angmen responded.

"That's so cool. Devin has a lot of parties too-" I should have bit my tongue. "Nooooooo! I should come to one! I've never gotten to see him use his famous snake powers," he said.

"Yeah! That would be awesome!" I said.

"So when is the next one?" he asked. Things escalated from there.

Not a week later I was back home and the "next one" was happening. It was a rager. Devin was extremely wasted. He was causing some of the invitees to levitate in the air of the hall and was performing all kinds of dangerous party tricks. In all honesty, I didn't expect Angmen to travel all the way from the east, but there he stood- in the doorway, shirtless. I was excited for a moment before I realized what was in his hand- an axe. Devin was sitting on his throne directly across from the entrance in which Angmen stood. He didn't notice the menacing figure until I shouted at him from the kitchen. Looking up from the woman giving him head, and seeing his uncle for the first time in years, he froze like a stone. The whole room froze. Everyone promptly parted down the middle making a clear path between the two relatives.

"Hey, Devin," Angmen said with a terrifying smile. "AAAAAAAAAAAAAAAAHHHHHHHHHHHH" said Devin while he rapidly flailed his arms

and legs. He kicked the woman away and tried to get up from his throne.

The small battle axe flew across the center of the room and planted itself in Devin's forehead. All the floating people fell to the floor and wine was spilled all over the place. I tried to kill Angmen. That's how I lost my left arm. He yanked the axe out of my best friend's head and swiftly used it to relieve me of my non-writing hand. Thankfully it was that one. Otherwise, these words may not be written down.

Angmen kicked Devin's body off the throne and climbed to the top of it. Standing above everyone, he shared a little speech.

"The House of Devin no longer exists, because Devin is forever dead. From now on, this kingdom will be known as The House of Angmen under the authority of Greenland Two. My first official act as king is to abolish Snakeism. You will no longer receive enough money to continue your nasty theatrical productions and wasteful parties. Oh, and if you would like to question my authority, you can either talk to my axe or the several thousand townspeople in the village below. They really seem to like my tax cuts... and what do you know? They also like me! Speak now if you don't *like* me and I would love to have a civilized discussion! But if you choose to act like this poor elderly goblin here, I will not be so civilized. I wish you all a pleasant evening. Drink your wine and revel in your debauchery. On the first of March I will appoint the next local governor based on the popular vote. Other than all that, you're all free to go about business as usual."

I'm now ninety-six writing this secret journal in a basement in someone's house in the woods outside the city limits on my deathbed. I write this, because the history books written during Angmen's rule are all faulty. They make Devin seem like a total villain. Children are taught that Devin enslaved thousands of people and made them worship him. It wasn't like that. I want the truth to exist somewhere. Even if it just sits in a box buried underground for a hundred years. Devin was not perfect, but he was a good king for those twenty five years. I still miss him every day. Before I pass into the next life I would like to write down the last song that I ever wrote.

I felt the green all over me.
Stone houses didn't seem
To catch me like the grass.

The thunder of a giant echoes
From the top of the highest mountain.
I remain fixed on a dandelion.
In the rain I revel in the smallness.

To those exalted and lofty,
Goodnight and farewell.
May your children prosper.

To those lowly and small,
Good morning and goodbye.
May you always stay beautiful.

The Mountain City of Rocky

My New Job

It had been about a hundred years since I became a forest-helper-person-friend to the gnomes. Humans were inevitably going to integrate into their culture at some point, so I decided to move north. I was still dead to humanity and I didn't want to hang out with anyone from Bird Land. I heard there was a city in the mountains ruled by giants (actual giants- not humans). I had to see it for myself.

Life changes too much to ever stay in the same place. I should have left earlier, but I wanted to help the gnomes as much as possible. Unfortunately, I reached a point where they began to think they were smarter than me. I didn't want to call them dumb, so I instead gave them what they all seemed to want most. I didn't fake my death this time. I just got on a horse and rode away.

I found the giant city. Its walls were probably a hundred feet high, and it was all made of stone. Before I made myself known to its people, I snooped around the city a bit. Their king truly was a giant. He was eight feet tall with a surprisingly aesthetic figure for someone so large. There was also a giant queen ruling by his side. She very much looked like a queen- more so than I ever could. I'm probably not ugly, but this woman was a towering sexy goddess.

Every building was brick and stone. Everything was tall with uniform designs. It was architecturally marvelous. I observed the behavior of the people there to be far less abrasive than that of Birdland's residents. Atmospherically, it was all very pillow-esque. They were eager to help with whatever I needed. It appeared that somebody was better than me at influencing their subjects. This wasn't necessarilly a mind-fucking revelation.

Before long, I found myself standing in the king and queen's court. Their names were Rocky and Busty. Their names were apt- hers even more so. I had never used that term...*busty*, in Shlangovia. That's when it dawned on me that Gavin had messed up pretty much every civilization in its infant stage. After some pleasantly brief exchanges with these dignitaries, I made the error of bringing up such a wretched topic.

"Do you guys know Gavin?"

Everyone in the court froze.

"Why would you assume that?" Busty asked.

"Oh shit," was my first thought. I came to learn that Gavin was widely known throughout the land. To humans, he was the devil. Apparently, to the giants, he was something even worse than that. They pulled me aside to explain that normal people don't talk about the things of the underworld so flippantly. They asked where I was from.

"I've lived among the gnomes for a long time. I recently decided to explore the world a bit. I heard about this city and it sounded quite cool," I said.

"It is very cool," Rocky said.

"Yeah. You will like it here. Are you an educated person?" Busty asked me.

"Actually, yes. I'm a bit of a scholar. I taught the gnomes a lot."

"That's very impressive. I didn't know gnomes could learn!" Rocky chuckled. I didn't find this jab to be humorous. Judging by the look she gave him, neither did Busty.

"I'm kidding. I love gnomes," he said nervously.

"Well, Apple... you've come at a convenient time. At your age, and with such evident sophistication, you strike me as more than qualified as a teacher. Our children- hell- our everyone is in dire need of wider knowledge about the universe. Do you specialize in math or maybe reading and writing?" she asked me.

"Everything. I specialize in everything," was my response. Cocky.

Before I knew it, I had become the local wise elder. People came to me from all over the kingdom to learn reading, writing, history, science, and arithmetic. Eventually, I ended up gaining significant publicity under this facade. People from all over the world traveled just to hear my teachings. I tried to keep my powers on the downlow, but I would slip up every now and then. Thankfully, those little mistakes only solidified the public opinion that Apple was fucking awesome. Over time, I became a highly respected figure in philosophy and... generally, everything. I remained in this position for close to fifteen hundred years.

When Busty and Rocky passed away it hurt a lot. They were one thousand years old and my closest friends at the time. Thankfully their son, Bert, took the throne. Bert was a bona fide genius in several areas. In the year 1000, on the day of his crowning, he appointed me to be his head advisor. We got along wonderfully.

Sisters of Sound
Hannah
Sarah
Saorsie

The Sisters of Sound

It was around the year 1030 when I met the Sisters of Sound. They came to The City of Rocky in search of places to perform. They were really the first popular band in Shlangovia and had been around for a few years. I had only heard them play once and I loved it. They could produce all kinds of majestic sounds out of thin air. They also invented woodwind instruments.

I attended their concert along with probably a couple thousand other people. Little did these three sisters know that their grandma was in the crowd. They were the princess daughters of my biological daughter: Magic Girl. Rumor had it that they hated their mom and everything about royalty. The sisters would later tell me that they disagreed with the general concept of hierarchy itself.

I gravitated strongly to these three beautiful beings. They were like soft wind. They did their thing and swept through the world leaving a gentle impression on the hearts of those who listened. I envied that energy. After the show, I approached them privately. I was feeling a lot of things, but guilt was at the top of the list. Their childhood trauma would have perhaps been evaded had I stayed to raise my own daughter. I didn't know that they had such trauma at that point, but I could see something familiar in their faces.

"Apple. We love you," one of them said. The other two just stared at me with their mouths slightly agape.

"I love you guys too. What are your names?" I asked. "I'm Sarah, this is Saorsie, and that's Hannah." "Your performance was amazing."

"We know. Your work is really good too," said Hannah.

"That's, like, the only reason we came here," said Sarah.

I wasn't sure if they knew who I really was. Part of me desperately wanted them to. The other part of me was terrified that they would react emotionally if they found out. I abandoned their mother and I still didn't know who raised her. This would be a reasonable cause for them to be very upset.

"What would you like to know, darlings?" I asked.

"We want to know more about you." I was too busy trying not to cry to figure out which one of them said that.

"You got me. Well, I'm Aife, your real grandma. I'm sorry I left your mom."

"We kind of already knew that, but don't worry about it," Sarah said while shaking nervously.

"We think that was a badass move," Hannah added, surprisingly composed.

"Wait- oh. I don't know about that," I said.

"It was. We've read about you. It's been made pretty damn clear that you probably weren't really dead. It's cool. You saw what you wanted and you went to get it- whatever it was. That's respectable. We've been trying to find you for decades," said Hannah.

"Well, thank you so much," I was running out of words. I was really happy.

The four of us talked for the rest of the night. They thought I was the coolest person to ever exist. Despite being renowned for their secrecy, they told me all about their lives. Their mom, Magic Girl, was raised by- you guessed it: one of Boby's whores! That specific whore was a very mean person and, subsequently, Magic Girl was abused as a child. I didn't like hearing this information, but I was too curious to stop them from sharing.

They grew up resenting her because she was extremely aloof and extra. She would have intense manic episodes where she would force all her subjects to attend her grand speeches. During these speeches she would talk for hours, but never say anything of substance. Everyone knew it was a call for help, but nobody could help her. At home, she would tell the sisters to behave a certain way and verbally assault them when they didn't. It made them especially bitter, because Magic Girl rarely ever abided by these obscure standards herself.

"Royal lines are bullshit," Saorsie said (the first thing I heard her say). Her sisters agreed. "One worm in the batch, and everything's fucking poisoned from that moment on,"

Hannah added.

"It's a generational curse. That's why we've all taken an oath," said Sarah. This oath essentially declared that none of the three sisters would ever marry, bear children, or accept their royal lineage as valid. I thought this was very extreme, given they had the potential to live for thousands of years.

"It's not extreme. We know that if we try to do any of those things, it will inevitably be fucked up. Trauma carries on down the family tree and it doesn't just disappear because you want it to," said Sarah.

Sarah was clearly the eldest, Hannah was the middle child, and Saorsie was the youngest. They all seemed to agree that music was their life. They only needed each other. The bond they shared was unbreakable. Their determination struck me as noble, but was it too much?

"Ladies, I'm fairly certain that everybody is generally fucked up. You can't let trauma define how you live your life. You may have to heal, but you have to let yourself be happy," I said. This was very two faced coming from me, but I still held it to be true.

"We know that. We are happy," said Hannah.

"We're happy enough. If we add crowns, husbands, kids or any of that shit, we won't be able to do all the things we truly enjoy. We might want those things from time to time, but that doesn't mean we need it, and it will probably just hurt us in the long run," said Sarah. This was a valid argument in my book.

Our conversations ensued well into the night. Some kind of deep connection occurred. I never expected to have grandchildren, let alone ones that liked me. It was one of the best feelings I'd ever experienced. I was never musical in the slightest, so I simply had to decline when they offered for me to tour with them. The sentiment alone made me sob. We ended the night all in each other's arms. It was probably the strangest family reunion I'd ever heard of. They agreed to tell nobody who I was.

The sisters stayed in my house for the next month and we all got to know each other very well. They loved King Bert and we all had a great time. They did about three shows in the city during this time. They all got pretty wild. I started to understand what they were saying. I was glad that they didn't want to have kids. It's not that I thought the sisters would be bad moms. It's just that the chances of bearing wizard children who don't use their powers for selfish gain is fairly low. They seemed happy enough without the burden of babies.

I cried when they left. They wanted to travel the world. They couldn't ever stay in one place for long. It was a damn shame. I really enjoyed their company. I can't blame them for my own instability, but my state of mind became rather dim without them.

Saorsie was the only one who ever came back to that city. She had broken her oath and been kicked out of the band. She was married to a wizard named Bill. Bill was Gavin's son. They had a child and named him Devin. It was close enough to 'Gavin' to honor the phonetics, but far enough to maintain individuality. Little Devin was a clever baby. I helped Saorsie and Bill raise him. Bill was very nice and he made Saorsie happy. That was good enough for me. The only major problem was that they both had now attained very demanding jobs. Bill was a top scribe, philosopher, and librarian who traveled constantly. Saoirse also travelled a lot. She had mastered the art of healing and monetized it. She went around to rich families who would pay her to heal their sick or wounded. Naturally, I was left to babysit Devin for a good chunk of his childhood. I taught him a lot of magic. That was probably a bad idea.

It was about this point in my life when I started to question my sense of moral responsibility. With so much power and influence, was I a bad person for not saving the world? I had heard about the wars and famine. I watched a child die once. I could have prevented a lot of disasters. I could have stopped all of it. Somehow, my experience with little Devin helped me process all this in a semi-healthy way. He was always getting into trouble. I was always there to help him be good. It often felt like I was, essentially, his mom. Years later, after Devin ran away, I learned that he became a con artist. As much as I disliked that, I was glad he didn't turn out homicidal, or worse. Saorsie and Bill did what they could, but there's only so much you can do when you have PTSD and are depressed- evidently suicidal on Bill's part. I envy normal wizards. They can live for thousands of years, but they aren't immortal. All that to say, I rest assured after that experience that I would never raise a child again.

I eventually ran out of reasons to stay in hiding. I was not fulfilling my purpose. At a certain point, I was too old to give a shit about what I wanted. Magic Girl's bastard son, Angmen, had conquered half the world by this point and was building an empire. The sisters didn't stop him. The mountain giants didn't stop him. Though many people could have, they didn't. Angmen was a psychotic murderer. Eventually he killed Devin, Sarah, and Hannah. He hated magic, even though he was a wizard. He despised kingdoms with progressive ideals. He was the quintessential fascist. His armies were unparalleled in size by the second millenia. Most cities and kingdoms that he besieged surrendered without a fight.

Under Angmen's reign, gnomes were enslaved. Humans would remove their incisors, so the gnomes couldn't use their venom. They were small and plentiful- viewed like rodents but with commercial purpose. Kingland was the world's first empire, and it was racist as fuck (among many other problematic things). It was founded on fear-mongering, violent force, and exploitation. This all happened before my very eyes while I did absolutely nothing.

I decided that I would return as Aife. I would conquer Kingland and kill Angmen. I needed to. Things had gotten out of hand. Maybe one of the mountain people could rule, or perhaps we would liberate the suffering kingdoms of the world. I needed time to prepare for this, so that's when Apple made that one infamous prophecy.

The ancient queen of everything
Does not like what she sees.

Evil doers prospering
And good people deceived.

She will rise from her slumber
And take back the world.

She will strike down the evil king
And free everybody.

ANGMEN

Most people laughed at me. Actually, this was widely considered a joke. I was just a strange old lady in the mountains going crazy. I didn't care. I knew everyone would believe it when they saw me "come back to life" and use my powers. Not long after the prophecy, Apple "died." In the year 1500, Aife rose from the dead. The generation that would have recognized my face had all died, but everyone believed it was me because of the prophecy.

I incited a revolution and killed Angmen. I claimed supreme leadership of Kingland. It was a shitty name, so I changed it to Wingland. First it was Greenland Two (probably something Gavin said), then Kingland, and since then, Wingland. My name for it was indisputably the best. Before long, I began expanding my empire. It stood for everything Angmen silenced. I began the long and grueling process of mass cultural reform. Taxes were lowered on the poor and the wealthy were put in check. I stripped back countless restrictions and laws. Gnomes finally started to have rights again. I destroyed the system that was in place and built it back from the ground up. I won't say that I was the best queen ever, but nobody really *has* to say that.

Magic Girl

The Family Reunion

Mom is getting better. I'm saying this because I think you should consider coming to the funeral. The reunion went a lot more smoothly than I expected- especially for Angmen being a murderous dictator now. I'm sure you'd rather not hear about any of this, but I'm gonna tell you, and you're gonna read every last word. Then, you can decide for yourself if you want to miss your own mom's funeral.

It was Bill, Saorsie, Devin, Angmen, mom, and me. As usual, none of us knew how we got there. We all woke up simultaneously sitting at the same old long stone table. At the end of it stood mom holding a wine glass in one hand and a cluster of grapes in the other.

"Hello, children," she said with that weird smile she does whenever she feels like a god. Devin slithered out of his chair and ran for the door. Mom caught him on the way and floated him back to the table (all without lifting a finger). Angmen wasn't excited to be there either.

"Mom, I'll fucking kill someone. I swear," he said. She just laughed.

"How? You're gonna outsmart me, honey?" she could barely articulate through her laughter.

"Is this really a good idea?" asked Bill.

"Nobody's getting hurt, honey. I'm in full control," Mom said.

"That's not what he meant," Saorsie chimed in.

"No. That is actually what I meant, but I'm still not convinced, Magic Girl." "I think *someone's* gonna get hurt," added Angmen as he glared at Devin.

"You think you got something on me, bitch? I accidentally killed a god. *A god.* And you have- abs. Ooh! You're so strong! The big man thinks he's immune to lightning! You know, for someone with a head as big as yours, your brain seems disproportionately miniature."

Once again, Mom averted an unwanted conflict. Angmen's fork was suspended midair above the center of the table, bound Devinward. She spoke as soon as it fell.

"You can fight after dinner, but no magic." she said. Devin broke out into a cold sweat upon hearing this.

"So, what are we gonna do? Are you planning on a big group hug or something? I hope you know that I don't intend on repairing any 'broken bonds.' Do you have alcho-" She interrupted Angmen. He yielded. You know he would have walked all over anyone else. I was a little surprised to see his respect for her still unfaltering.

Bill

Saorsie

Devin

Angmen

Magic
Girl

Sarah

"We're going to eat. Then, we're going to talk about our lives. After that, we'll have dessert while you and Devin fight."

Everyone looked at each other and non verbally agreed that there was nothing we could do to stop this from happening. Some of us were enemies, some of us were estranged, and some of us used to be in a band, but like we've always done, we had our family reunion.

Seeing Devin was really nice. He was pouting for the first ten minutes, but I cheered him up. I'm not mad at Saoirse anymore. I don't think she ever wanted to be a part of the band in the first place. She's just trying to find herself, and Bill is part of that process. I personally want Bill and Devin to feel welcome in our family regardless of what has happened in the past. In all honesty, I think this was a very good thing for everyone.

"How have you been, Devin?" Saorsie asked. Devin shuddered as he does when his mom asks him personal questions.

"I mean- it's- it's going fine. I'm making a lot of money."

Anytime she comes into the picture, he's like a tiny child again. To me, he's always been a kid running away. Aren't we all? We ran away from mom, Saorsie ran from us, and Devin ran from Saorsie. It's a cycle that can't be broken. No matter how much self-awareness we possess, we just can't beat our family tradition. That being said, a lot happened that night that genuinely touched me. It's hard to explain.

The conversations became more friendly as the night went on. In fact, Angmen and Bill made each other laugh quite a bit. For once, mom didn't try to censor the conversations or control the tone. I think she'd grown a lot. For her to just sit there without interjecting for more than five minutes indicated that she had learned more about herself.

When I asked her why she didn't bring you, she said it's because you hate her. I know that's not true, but she never found that out. It's nothing to be ashamed of on your part. I just wish we could have all been there one last time. I know she hurt you the most. Even if you did hate her, I would understand. You don't know how much it would mean to me, Saorsie, Bill, and Devin for you to come to the funeral next week. That's right; I included Devin. Even he is coming.

"Do you feel strong, Devin?" asked Angmen while he picked the steak out of his teeth.

"I don't feel anything," Devin grunted. Mom tried to subtly escalate. "Devin, if you don't want to fight, that's ok. He is a lot stronger than you." "There's no shame in it, son. I don't think anyone here would stand a chance ag-"

Angmen interrupted Bill.

"It's okay if you're scared of me, Devin."

We could all feel the tension as testosterone flooded the room. After a frightening pause, Mom suggested they just have their fight then and there- in the dining hall. None of us stood up to watch. You know how it goes. This time, things got bad very fast. The last time they did this, they were teenagers and things were a lot more playful. This one went a little too far.

After circling each other and hurling elementary insults, Devin sent one solid punch into Angmen's nose. It broke. On the first hit, his nose broke. We all heard it. They kept circling nonetheless.

"Come on, you little bitch. Come on you fucking- fucking assh-"

Angmen cut him off with two blows to the gut. Devin took that opportunity to deliver an uppercut. Angmen twisted Devin's arm around and kicked in his knees. With his arm locked, Devin was on his knees facing away while Angmen pulled his hair and laughed- all with blood streaming out of his nose. Saorsie begged mom to call it off, but she wouldn't budge.

Devin somehow maneuvered himself so his entire body ascended up Angmen's arm in a kind of backwards somersault. That's how strong Angmen is now if you can imagine. He held Devin suspended in the air with one arm. However, the consequence of this weird move was not anticipated.

Devin's balls landed directly on Angmen's mouth as Devin locked himself around his head. Angmen ran around the room knocking Devin into walls and slamming him into the floor. All the while, his screams were being muffled by the lightly clothed genitals and ass pressing against his face. Devin was still laughing while his ribs were being broken. Mom was going to fix them all up afterwards, so she didn't feel the need to stop it.

Angmen was now begging for her to call off the fight. Unfortunately, Bill, her, and I were all too busy laughing to hear his pleas. Angmen's weakness is genitalia. That just so happens to be Devin's super power. Finally, Devin lost his grip and was flung across the room into a shelf.

Precious glass dishes fell on him. Angmen's face was completely red, most likely from embarrassment. He ran to the table and snatched a steak knife. Right as he coiled his arm for the throw, Mom froze him in place. The laughing stopped. Angmen was a split second away from killing Devin. Mom took Angmen to another room to reprimand him. Devin chuckled to himself in a pile of broken glass. She did, in fact, save his life that day. That's probably why he's coming to the funeral.

Just think, Hannah; this is the worst thing that happened and mom had barely anything to do with it! In her mind, they needed to let out that aggression. I just might agree with her. It all ties back in with my tradition spiel. They've been fighting since they were toddlers. Only now has it gotten out of hand, because they're actually men. And guess what: mom announced that fighting was no longer allowed at the reunions. Like, duh, but also that was a really big step for her! I don't know. I just hope you know that she cared about you. Hurting the people you love the most is a real thing, because deep down you don't want them to leave you behind. I just don't want you to think that she didn't love you.

There's been a lot- too much. There's been too much pain in our family, and I could see it in everyone during that dinner. Angmen could barely look at Mom without his eyes starting to water. Saoirse and I hugged for the first time in probably thirty years. Bill did everything he could to lighten the mood when things got heated. Though he would never admit to this, I think Devin started to see how much he values all of us. On top of everything, nobody treated Mom like a crazy person. For once, we all respected her mental illness and she was happy as hell to see everyone interacting as normally as possible. It seems like our family was just starting to work in a weird way. I don't write this to make you feel bad. I just want you to know that I miss you. I don't care if you did something bad. I don't care if you're angry at me. I just want to see you. If it has to be our mother's funeral, that's alright with me. I love you, Hannah.

—Sarah

The Funeral

Sarah, I get it. Just because she was evil and twisted and author-itarian doesn't mean she was technically a stone cold sociopath with genuinely no feelings. I'm glad to know that you've only now realized that she is in fact, a human. You're allowed to be ok with honoring her death. I personally am not. She didn't hate you, so why should you hate her? The highest honor I can allow myself to bestow upon her is to not hate her. That's all she gets from me. All I got from her was hate. Also, I don't give a shit what was in the will. Even if she left me ten cities, you can deal with them. I don't need anything else from her and she never needed anything from me. You're also very right about having no idea what I went through. That should have been enough to indicate that you have no room to request my presence at an event at which her praises will be sung. With love, fuck off.

-   Hannah

[Crucial Information from Elijah]

There are certain things that I feel are somewhat pressing for the reader to know in order to fully appreciate these stories. Their authors had a tendency to sidestep details that were common knowledge in Shlangovia, but otherwise unknown on earth. That's why I'm interjecting.

First off, I'd like to address the public perception of wizards in this world. It was largely dependent on the time period. During the first millenium, generally everybody knew who Aife and her descendants were. Anyone from that lineage inherited stardom upon birth.

As for Gavin, the world knew he existed for a while. Due to lack of physical proof, everyone eventually came to believe he wasn't real. By the third century of the second millenium, almost nobody (save for the goblin people) believed he was a legitimate historical figure. Gavin's grandson Devin had so many children that eventually being a wizard was just kind of a thing. Shlangovians never realized that wizard genes were strictly hereditary. Devin's fruitfulness aided in creating the illusion that just about any baby conceived by a human could turn out to have magical tendencies.

Gavin's descendents weren't very powerful. Devin's great - grandchildren weren't taught how to harness their abilities, or really tap into them. This eventually resulted in most wizards being regarded as just weirdos who lived long. The most powerful wizards were always subtle about their use of magic. Harnessing nature is a tremendous moral weight, so they often opted to do so quite sparingly. Gavin was the exception to this. He was not afraid to show off to his people.

On the flip side, when two well - learned, full - blooded wizards mate, their child will, more often than not, grow to be ridiculously overpowered. This brings me to the basic explanation of wizardry which I will try to sum up in just a few paragraphs.

Just about anyone can become a wizard. You have to know and understand yourself and your surroundings extremely well. Magic is sort of a way of "hacking" into the fabric of physical reality. It may take you eighty years of intense practicing and dedication before you have anything to physically show for it. Only when you've reached the maximum human extent of self-awareness and understanding of the physical realm, can you begin to shift the world around you. At least, this is generally the case.

I've had several students master the art in only twenty years and still be absolute twats. It simply depends on the person and how connected their soul is to everything. Some people are just disconnected from the physical world and could never be a wizard. It requires vast levels of harmony to everything and everyone. That's why there has never been a sociopathic wizard with any luck at mastering their powers. Angmen tried to convince everyone he did not need magic, but the truth was, he was terrible at it. Empathy is one of the most crucial pillars to stable wizardry. Gavin would have disagreed. He didn't believe himself to be very empathetic, but he was.

What about all those small, hairy, buff mountain people from the first chapter? Well, they retreated into the mountains far north. Their population only decline from twenty - four. The lifespan of a mountain person was a thousand years, but they could only produce one offspring during that time. By the third millennium, there were only six left. Many of them became great rulers of human kingdoms. The ones that did exist in the public eye were widely respected. Some chose to live isolated in giant mountain halls. All the mountain people were at least seven feet tall when full grown and they were all inhumanly strong. In battle, they were unrivaled.

Aife always worked very closely with the mountain people. She had two of them on her high council of rulers in Wingland. Despite this, Aife would secretly meet up with Gavin every hundred years, give or take. You have to understand, mountain people always remembered Gavin. When the whole world forgot about him, they only grew more furious. Aside from the dark, exaggerated campfire stories, they were genetically predisposed to hate Gavin. They didn't need a reason to feel this way.

The following content is arguably very boring. You can skip this section of the book if you'd like.

Kingland was the greatest empire to exist until Aife rose up. Down the road, once Angmen had more power than any man before him, he decided to do a crusade of sorts into the south. In South Shlangovia there was some desert where the goblin - humans lived. This was as far away from humans as they could get. They never bothered anyone, but due to their ugliness and generally perceived inferiority, Angmen campaigned to wipe them out. Unfortunately, he succeeded.

Angmen didn't truly hate his family. He refused to kill Magic Girl (his mom) or Saoirse (his half sister). The only reason he killed Apple and Hannah was because they were avid protestors during his rule. They led riots into the Capitol and even attempted to overtake his personal palace with a group of revolutionaries. In his defense, they were total bitches to him his whole life.

Magic Girl was killed in a riot in the year 1909. Ironland was the only kingdom Angmen never touched, but after his mother's passing, he seized control of it.

Since the beginning of his rule, Gavin continued to expand the underworld and help the goblin population thrive. The goblins respected him like a god and would do anything he asked them to. That's why a lot of inventors found their work randomly demolished. When Gavin didn't approve of something new, he would have his spies go out and see to its destruction. He didn't allow certain things to exist that he deemed "terrible and stupid." Such inventions were plastic, electricity, anything remotely similar to the game of basketball, books about sex, and processed meat. His beliefs were rather arbitrary in every sense.

Goblin spies were sometimes caught and interrogated. Some of them eventually gave in and admitted that Gavin was their superior, but nobody up top ever seeked revenge. Why?

There was once a rather detrimental game of telephone amongst the goblin military leadership. One goblin clan pillaged an entire human city. They didn't just rob it. They killed nearly every person inside without a trace. They snuck over the walls in the middle of the night and slit the people's throats. They killed any man, woman, and child they could find.

This massacre was in response to a goblin child being beaten to death in the city street. The large-scale ambush that ensued was primarily an act of direct retaliation, but a lot of people wondered if it also had to do with hundreds of years of racial descrimination and oppression building up.

After the bloodbath, all humans realized that they were truly no match for goblins in any combat scenario. They were also twice as fast as normal humans, nearly impervious to physical pain, and they could see perfectly in almost pitch black. If you made a goblin mad, you were told to only sleep during the day. Gavin never condoned violence, but the human/gnome world was not necessarily aware of this. After the raid (which happened sometime in the 1800s) it became widely agreed upon that Gavin was a homicidal villain. Despite being understood as a threat, goblins were continuously viewed as inferior, corrupted creatures by gnomes and humans alike. This racism carried on from the beginning of time and into the last days.

Goblin skin is quite pale and would burn terribly if they stood in the sun for very long. This is why they naturally thrived in mountains and caves. Very little social or cultural interaction ever occurred between gnome colonies, goblin clans, and human governments. Though the three races would intermingle in cities like Birdland and Rome, each race tended to adhere to their own sector.

I feel bad for jumping in right in the middle of the chronological timeline. I hope it doesn't throw off the pace. There's a lot more that I'd like to address, but I'll spare you. Continue.

I Hate the Queen

This is an incomplete passage from a letter written by a gnome named Darrel. He was presumably writing this letter to his girlfriend when he suffered a stroke and died in his house.

My dearest Tabitha, forgive my bluntness, but you don't know the first thing about politics. Please don't try to outwit me. You just can't. I've dedicated my thirties to educating myself as much as possible. Not to be rude, but you aren't exactly the most learned person. That's not to discount your parent's financial disposition. Some people are simply more privileged than others. I happen to be fortunate enough to travel abroad.

First off, you're wrong about Queen Aife. Dead wrong. I think it's easy to see her as some heroic figure, but that's her goal. Your entire region is impoverished simply because she refuses to integrate legitimate democratic policy into the provincial governments. You complain about such high taxes, but maintain that Queen Aife is the patron saint of equality. She knows about your suffering, but instead of tending to the ailments of her people, she'd rather go to war with the closest country to her borders. She has no reason to conquer the kingdoms of the south, but she's doing it anyway. Why? Because she's a power - hungry, greedy, nasty leader.

Wingland is not currently (and never has been) free from racism or inequality. Sure- on paper, Aife freed gnomes and gave us "equal rights" but that doesn't mean anything when the entire political system that she governs practically runs on subjugation and exploitation. She calls it a republic, but technically it's an empire.

Notice how people literally have to storm the Capitol in a riot in order for any legitimate change to take place. She will only adhere to what the people want when it's in her own best interest.

Bear in mind that she has consistently gone against her own peace treaties when she feels it is convenient. Her intentions are to literally rule the world. Does that notion alone feel right to you? Does a supreme council of a hundred people sound any better? They all have the exact same goals, because they're addicted to this particular status quo. They live in the largest castles on the most expensive mountains. The normality we know today is arguably *worse* than the feudalism she vowed to abolish. At least citizens were protected from violence then! Our own knights are currently at liberty to physically strike people down without cause. Yes, it's illegal, but there are no penalties for those who abuse their power. Under Aife, free speech is a hypothetical reality. Whereas under a different leadership model, it would be entirely achievable.

DARREL

You aren't naturally inclined to regard anything I say as valid, because you've been conditioned to this system. Despite its claims, it allows no room for genuine free thought. If you even imply that gnomes are still suffering, you're automatically insulting the queen. When you insult the queen, you're effectively blacklisted by your community. When you're blacklisted you can't work, so you beg for money at the city gates. When you're ostracized by the very people you're begging from, guess what? THEY WON'T HELP YOU! So you die of diseases or starvation.

Aife just dodges these issues with fallacies and by waving around the phrase "the council is tending to-." How do we know what the council is doing and not doing? They've never been transparent! They only share whatever is most "pressing." Emphasis on the "pressing" bit. Darling, we are being boiled like frogs.

Just because she's thousands of years old doesn't mean her intentions are pure. If anything, she's had plenty of time to learn people's behavior and manipulate the general population into being her mindless puppets. Nobody even questions that the theater societies are predominantly government owned and operated. The very plays we watch are supposed to ingrain her ideals into our minds. We've all been indoctrinated.

Did you know Aife literally has trophy skulls? If so, please don't tell me you think that's okay. Those are people that she KILLED. For someone as pro-pacifism as her, she seems determined to always be killing people. She won't allow room for civil interactions with monarchies or even other republics if they dare to refuse her rule. You have to realize how wrong this is. She is forcing everyone to be her bitch. I know this may be difficult for you to comprehend, but people can do a lot of bad things in the name of good things.

I hope you understand that my intention isn't to berate you or make you feel stupid. Though it is understandable if you do feel stupid. Just know that this woman is not your hero. She doesn't care about you and will not fight for you any further. I know you love peace, equality, and overall acceptance of everyone, but you have to understand that Aife does not.

If after reading this, you still claim that she is "amazing," I will be forced to question your intelligence. If you don't believe me on any of these issues, just find out for yourself. There is a library in your district. Go there and see for yourself. Ask a historian. Don't be dense, Tabitha. Don't fall for the big trick. I'm sure you're smarter than that. I also think you need to consider eating less. I'm coming to see you in May and I want

Captain Kennedy's Secret

I certainly wouldn't call myself a humble man. For the majority of my life, I've felt rather proud of my accomplishments. I've sailed around the world, led two successful conquests, and been happily married for almost a decade. Though it might seem wrong to certain narrow minded individuals, I'm very pleased with who I am. But this story isn't about me. It's about something that I don't like. I possess a certain dangerous knowledge of an ungodly nature. If you're reading this, you have dug this document up from underneath a special rock in my backyard. Good job. Now enjoy, as you read this unsettling, forbidden text.

I am a general, ambassador, knight, and explorer for the queen of Wingland. I have known her for years and we have always maintained a pleasantly professional relationship. I've served her diligently and now operate on a very close level to her. In fact, I am one of her most trusted officials. That's why this is a very difficult situation. I'm tempted to forget everything I saw, but if I don't write it down, it will continue to run around in my brain. It tortures me. I need some kind of release; even if it's through my mere pen. I told my best friend, Bear, but he has this way of making one feel small when speaking. I didn't even finish the story, because he was fuming in anger. I knew he wouldn't tell a soul. He's not the type to involve himself in royal drama. Aside from him, you (whoever that may be) may now be the first to feast your eyes on this disgusting revelation.

Let me take a moment to describe Queen Aife'sofficial throne room in Bird City. The ceiling has to be over two hundred feet high.

Barely anyone has been in there. It ascends heavenward in a narrow hall. It's adorned with artesian tapestries and various flowery designs. The windows allow a lot of sunlight to enter. There are a lot of plants. The floors are marble. Sorry if at any moment, my recollections lose coherency. I'm drinking right now as I write. You can't blame a man for coping the only way he might know how.

There are never guards in there. She seems to always be engaged in discussion with at least two or three other dignitaries. This giant hall is basically her office. I like how she never makes us bow. She treats everyone the same. When I last visited her in Bird City, I was trying to tell her about my strategy for efficient law enforcement in the southern isles. She pretended to be interested, but she appeared to be more invested in her other guest's remarks about the furniture. She dismissed me, so I started to walk out- rather annoyed that she did not pay me much attention. Then, to my shock, she yelled for me to halt. I did.

THE CAPITAL of WINGLAND-
BIRD CITY

"Wait! Why don't you just join us for dinner, Kennedy?" she asked. I was flattered to be offered such a privilege, so I sat down at her stone table. It was the largest table I've ever seen. It was long, rectangular, and depicted vineyards and poems on every side. The cooks brought us exotic food. It was a very cool dinner. Aife's eyes were bouncing between me and the two others present, carefully spending the proper amount of time on each person according to who was speaking at the moment. As the night went on, everyone kept drinking. It had already been two hours or so. I was worried about my wife getting worried.

Everyone gradually unfolded over the course of the evening. I felt pressure to stay, because Aife wouldn't leave me alone. We were so drunk, somehow she ended up lying sprawled on the floor with her face buried in my belly. I was very confused and a little worried. It was all a bit of a haze. One of the other guests broke a priceless vase by kicking it across the room. Aife didn't let the minstrel stop playing this entire time. It was the five of us sitting around in her royal throne room; stumbling and mumbling about obscure things. I was too shocked to question anything. I remember waking up from a brief nap to see one of the guests dancing on top of the table and kicking the fruit in different directions. Apparently they were a very wealthy local couple. I think their names were Harold and Amy or something. They were too busy partying to pay attention to what Aife was about to tell me.

She lifted her head off my stomach and looked me straight in the eye. She was laughing more than I had seen her ever laugh before. I was scared. She said something like,

"You know Kennedy, I fucking hate all of this. I'm into art and shit, you know? I'm really fucking old, but I can still fuck whoever I want... and I do. I'm like more of a *fucking* queen than I am a wizard queen. You know, everyone hates me and I'm ugly. I know this because they- they get like a surge of power when they know they're doing something wrong. I'm rich, I'm powerful. For some men, that's more enticing than tits. I don't think anybody is genuinely attracted to my physical body. How would I know though? You know? Ugh. I love you, Kennedy. You're like a younger brother to me. Can I tell you a secret?"

I felt awful for enabling her divulgence in such a compromised state, but I was too terrified to deny her request.

"Ok. I trust you, man. I really really trust you. Like you're one of the only cool generals I know. That's why I'm telling you this."

There was a long pause only to be broken by her belch.

"I'm like, in love with the King of the Underworld. You know the goblin king, Gavin? I love him. I want to like, hold his hand and sleep with him and shit. Yeah. I'm messed up. I'm really messed up, damnit! Fuck. I'm sorry, Kennedy. You're the only person who knows! Shhhhh. You know, if people find out, cities will burn, people will die, and someone will- the council will inevitably take me down. But, what people don't realize is that he's not even a bad guy! He's just trying to do the best he can for his people. He's not a genius by any means. Maybe he's a little confused sometimes, but I don't want a genius! I want a good guy. I want a genuinely nice motherfucker to fuck me. My husband is a greedy little bitch- just like every guy I've ever married. I don't care- I don't care if he hears me say that. If he somehow doesn't leave me, I'll outlive him anyway. You know, I'm so fucked up right now. I'm so fucked up right now. I'm so fucked up that like- at least once a week I will climb to the top of the toppest of the tip of the tallest tower in the palace, and jump off. Yeah. My body gets destroyed and I'm like basically dead for a second, but then it all just heals right up. I'm not kidding. I want to die so bad. What the hell kind of *blessing* is this? I just want him. I wa- people. My people are my priority obviously, but mainly, I want to be with Gavin. I want to be with him so damn bad."

I was unable to process this disturbing avalanche of information.

"He had this giant Scottish sword he told me about a couple centuries back. He lost it at some- I want that sword. I want his sword. I want him to penetrate me. I want his big cock sword to cut me into a million pieces. I want hi- what the fuck am I saying? HA! Ha. I need help, Kennedy. Not that you're not helping. You really are.

I don't like- really like therapy so this is really good for me. Oh my god I love him so much."

At this point her arms were wrapped around me and my shirt was wet from her tears. I didn't want to push her away and offend her, but in respect for my wife I kindly asked that she release me from her grip. She did. Then she apologized in probably ten different ways. I told her it was ok, but I was concerned.

The queen of Wingland herself admitted to me that she wanted to have sex with the devil. Gavin is a secretive ruler, but the high council knows a lot about his workings. I will just say that he is not as noble as she made him out to be. There is a reason why technological progress has been suspiciously halted in the cities. Almost every night, somewhere in Shlangovia, blueprints are burned, inventions are smashed, statues are toppled, diagrams go missing, etcetera. We have reason to believe that the goblins who commit these vandalous acts of destruction are under his service. His intent is to halt all progress and to corrupt any beauty that he sees unfolding in the world. I believe it is because deep down, he is jealous. According to history, no human has seen his face in thousands of years, but Aife clearly had. It's reasonable to assume that he is the most ugly person in the world. I'm basing this assumption on Aife's failure to at any point mention a notable physical attribute of his; except for his cock. I digress.

I walked alone through the city at eleven pm and stumbled into my house. My wife was asleep. I fell to the floor and dreamed about my homeland burning.

For the next few weeks, this strange truth was all I could think about. It bothered me a lot. I'm actually still bothered. I love the queen, but she is clearly not well. For the good of the kingdom, I am torn between notifying the council, and letting this secret die in my backyard. Oh shit. I am immoderately vexed.

I respect Aife. She's the most capable leader I've ever seen. I could never personally see to her defamation. However, for the good of the world, I am forced to question my undying allegiance to her. She wasn't lying that night. There were very real feelings in her face.

She confronted me the following day to inform me that such a sentiment is ludicrous. She told me she was kidding about all that. The queen could never love the devil! Yeah. It was bullshit. For a moment I was tempted to buy it. She made it so convincing that I was almost capable of rearranging my memory of the night to fit her explanation. I was snapped out of that fantasy when she started to stutter through her words and abruptly walk away. Her sense of humor could never deteriorate to such a tasteless extent.

Whatever. This is all just here. I don't want to ruin her reputation. I don't want to further fuck the economy or the already tense, sociopolitical climate. It's already bad enough in Bird City. I just have to get it out of me somehow. I'm not really a writer and I might never do this again, but this is better than nothing. I am torn. Who can I trust if not the great wizard queen herself? It is safe to say that ever since this experience, I have perceived the world through a rather poorly lit, foggy lense. That's it. That's all. I'm worried. There's no moral here. I just had to get this off my chest. I hope someone reads this one day. Or maybe this paper will decompose after a hundred years... Maybe this will be forever unknown as a minor hiccup in an otherwise successful reign.

Gavin and Aife Pt. 1

I have dedicated a sad amount of my lifetime to choking out my feelings for Angela/Aife/Apple. She's nothing like me and we have very little in common. She's never been good at communicating how she feels. It doesn't make sense for us to date. As anything more than distant friends, we've always been prone to being inherently emotionally hurtful to each other. I've spent centuries seething with anger for her. I've spent other centuries infatuated with her. It's tragic, but this obnoxious cycle is shared by both of us. Though unfortunately, it's never been synced up.

Over the course of history, we have rarely ever been in love with each other at the same time. We've gone through several eras where the lines of how we truly felt were blurred by carnal passion. She's probably pity-fucked me more times than I'd like to know. We've had a lot of angry sex too. We've never waged war on each other, but it came close once or twice. She's always been off and on. I've always loved her, but that's not to say I haven't also hated her at times.

Several weeks ago there was a bit of a turning point in our relationship. We were supposed to meet in my vacation cabin at eleven pm sharp. As far as I knew, she wanted me to help her solve a rioting crisis or something. For a long time up until that night, I was under the impression that anything romantic or sensual between us was over. We had both moved on. Things were looking up for our professional relationship going forward. I had thought this several times before, and it was always wrong.

By twelve thirty, she still hadn't shown up. Queens aren't late, so I assumed she was trying to make a point. Feeling cheated, my accompanying friends and I realized that we needed to have a guy party. There was a lot of rum, it was raining outside, and I had my flute. We danced around, talked about guy stuff, drank, and played throw the looser. That's my favorite drinking game. To a goblin, if you get to play 'throw the loser,' it basically means you're officially friends with me. They can't play the game without me, because they can't throw each other like I can. It's also illegal for anyone to play it without me.

I was like "Fuck her. We can have a good time." I was right- but in a different way than I meant to be. She showed up around one o' clock. Her hair and clothes were singed and there was all kinds of shit on her. After Mr. Douglass reluctantly let her in, she glared at me. She didn't say very much. It was an amazing sight. She seemed humiliated by trying so hard to not be humiliated by five drunk idiots. According to her, the gods struck her with lightning. I believed her, but it was hilarious nonetheless.

With some subtle facial communication, she made it clear to me that she didn't want to talk with my friends in the room. Once they vacated, she started telling me how much she loved me. I considered this to be very disrespectful. All of those years trying to move on- now wasted as I looked into her infinite eyes. I was angry enough to throw a table at her, but I felt bad enough for her to not do that. I almost did though. I was drunk. She said a lot. As it turns out, she was pretending to be over me for a long time. I genuinely had gotten over her, but it was all rushing back like a dam being broken by a raging storm. Again, I was mad, but seeing her tears welling up and realizing how dire everything was, it hit me that nothing matters. I was drunk. All I remember is that we had really good sex in a very small amount of time. Everything from there is rather foggy.

After that night, we had a few secret meetups- dates, if you will. For a brief speck of our lives, we were fully, mutually, madly in love. We were also happy. I know she wasn't faking it. She didn't have a reason to. If she would've been caught by anyone, the high council would've found out and they would've tried to imprison her or worse.

It's not against the law to go on secret dates with the devil, but if you do, everyone will hate you and you're certainly not fit to be a queen. Every human and gnome likes Aife. Every human and gnome except for Aife, hates me. That is the unchanging certainty of my life.

Unfortunately, I'm part of the world- which is who she recently decided to ghost entirely. She completely disappeared from the public eye. As one can rightly assume, I was slightly put off by this decision. For once, we had something nearly perfect going. Then, with no explanation, she left me. It's a bad move. I'm fairly certain that I will never speak to her again even if she wants to. I'm fucking done. I've been through enough love. I don't need any more of it. If she wants to be a jerk, that's absolutely fine. She's entitled to be whatever she wants to be. However, I feel wronged just enough to rightfully say that she's a bitch. She's a bitch. She's a cold hearted, spoiled, childish, bitch girifhkjiiefblosddadfkxcbnyewabkdvkmlkbolsdvlkieoosojfjy-wdkgilsiefnsilejvlsvn FUCKING FUCK. WHY DOES EVERYONE LIKE HER SO MUCH?! GOD! SHE'S SO ANNOYING!

Gavin and Aife Pt 2

The Meeting

I think there was one night of my life where everything kind of lined up in a way that I felt was… fairly perfect. It happened two nights ago and I need to write it down before I forget the details. Bear in mind that you (the reader) are nobody. You don't exist. However, I like to entertain myself, so I will write as if you do.

My good friend Bear (one of the few mountain people left) started acting strange one day, saying he had to go on a "quest". He didn't tell me what it was about, but I knew it had something to do with Captain Kennedy. They were looking over at me and whispering to each other at a banquet the other night. I swear, if Kennedy told Bear about my outburst I am going to temporarily nullify my anti-death sentence order. Just kidding. I would just hire an assassin. That's besides the point. What is the point? Oh yeah! I got pretty lonely when Bear left.

I decided to go on a little road trip to Rocky City. That's where Saorsie still lives. Honestly, I just wanted to have tea with her. Well, I got a little more than that. She went on and on about how she had fallen in love with this girl. This was very interesting to me. Not that she was bisexual, but that she was spilling her guts so profusely. It seemed like as the centuries passed, and she got to know me, she became increasingly more comfortable expressing herself in small doses. But that day, she did not stop. This is the girl who rarely says a single thing in public. She's known for being perpetually silent. I just sat and listened to her spill. It surprised me, but I wanted to hear it all.

"She takes me to the river and we just look at fish. They're just fish, but it's such a cute moment. We spend pretty much every day together. We held hands last Tuesday night. That probably sounds like nothing to you, but it was something for me. She's the first person who likes me and understands me- besides you of course. But do you know what that's like? Having someone that you know could make your life infinitely happier? She's distantly related to me, but fuck it, you know? We're not gonna have a kid."

This pretty much sums up the extent of content within our conversation. She continued on for a while about how happy she was.. It had a deep effect on me. For once, I barely said a word during our exchange. I was more than okay with that. However, I was getting a little jealous of her. It made me happy to know she had something so pure in her life, but as anyone would, I wanted it for myself.

She just so happened to fall in love with another wizard, and that wizard was inconsequentially able to spend every day with her. I didn't need to, but I started to re-evaluate my definition of happiness- more so, the value of it. Would a happy queen make a better one? I had a lot of feelings that I wasn't allowing room for. It really hurt. At this point, I was certain that just about anything would be a good idea- as long as it got me off my ass and into something that I *actually* cared about. So, I set up a meeting.

I came alone as usual. It was storming like a bitch and I wasn't convinced that the gods weren't going to smite me. The lightning was gradually growing uncomfortably closer. For some reason, it dawned on me only halfway through my trip that my moose could run. No sooner than that idea popped up, the aforementioned moose and I were struck by lightning.

Having been knocked out for god knows how long, I awoke with most of my blood-stained clothing either blackened or disintegrated. My poor ride, who I forgot the name of, was not in prime condition. His head was literally gone and his blood had been totally cauterized at the neck. Soaked, annoyed, tired, hungry, thirsty, bitter, and horny- I decided to sprint the rest of the way to Gavin's house. Yes. He does have a house. Nobody knows about it except for me... and of course several goblins.

I slipped in the mud a few times. At this point, I was almost certain that Gavin wouldn't be interested in doing anything naughty. I looked worse than *he* did on a normal day. That's hard to do.

I looked up. At the top of a hill in the middle of the woods was that beautiful savior of a log cabin. The soft lantern light fell only a few feet out of the windows before it was vanquished by the rain. I could faintly hear the sound of a flute and some singing. Shadows danced enough for me to notice them from out the windows. There were definitely more than a couple people in there. I did not anticipate this at all.

I knocked on the door. The goblin who opened it seemed put off that I had dared interrupt his partying. He didn't even act surprised to see the queen herself covered in mud, blood, and wearing burnt clothes, showing up at the Lord of the Underworld's secret cabin secretly in hopes of possibly fucking his brains out. I suppose Gavin was just trying to have a good time. Evidently, we had a conflict of interests.

"You here for Gavin?" he asked shortly after downing a mug of rum while I stood in the rain.

"Yeah. Can I come in, man?" I asked; poorly attempting to disallow a rude tone.

"Gavin's not here, bitch." Either this young goblin had no brain, or he wanted to die. Lucky for him, I didn't have to decide which one it was, because Gavin saved his ass.

"Come on, Clancy! Let her in for shit's sake!" he shouted from within the wooden walls. Clancy (that stupid bitch) slowly let the door open just enough for me to squeeze in. See, I can't call people stupid bitches publicly. I can't even call people that to my friends. That's why I need this journal. That's why I need *you.*

I entered the single room house to see four or five young goblins who had abruptly stopped dancing. Directly across from me sat Gavin. He was holding a flute and wearing those stupid fucking footy pajamas. He always tries to start crazy fashion trends by blatantly ripping off old earthian clothes. It just devalues- nevermind. This story gets better. I promise.

"Oh shit. What happened to you?" Gavin asked. There were a lot of automatic responses that I had to avoid vocalizing in order to maintain the probable chance that he would be interested in interacting with me on a physical level.

"I think the gods struck me with lightning. Then I started running and I slipped in mud."

Gavin is easily entertained. Not only him, but all his little friends found this concise recollection humorous enough to end up rolling on the floor.

"My moose died," I said, hoping it would be a show stopper. Nope. This only heightened their uproar (which one would assume to be physically impossible).

"I'm sor- I- I'm I'm so-HGGHEYAEAAAAAAAH," said Gavin with the temperament of someone unqualified to be a king.

Even Clancy was laughing his ass off. They wouldn't stop. The collective endorphins in the room were enough to make me forget that I was annoyed. I cracked a smile. Apparently that was the least funny thing I'd done thus far. At that point, everybody calmed down.

"So, Aife... we were gonna talk about the riots and stuff, right? The Nectar District isn't doing too hot."

Gavin was very drunk. I wanted to match the energy, so I downed two bottles of... something.

"I don't want to talk about policy."

"Well, there's the Bridgepoint Revolution- if you can call it that. I could have my boys go in and shut everyone up pretty quickly. I know your hands are full. I imagine you don't have many troops to spare. You know we could come up with a lot of narratives for this one. I mean, it's a bunch of kids with sticks breaking shit. I doubt the public would be too upset if-"

He looked up and realized the look I had been giving him for the duration of his spiel. It was my we-need-to-talk-privately look. We have a lot of looks that we both know.

"Oh. I see. You want to talk about the dog overpopulation issue in Rome. Ok, boys? I'm gonna need you all to step outside for this one. There are a lot of ins and outs," he said.

It wasn't a very convincing cover up, but they promptly obeyed without complaining. Gavin never intentionally used fear tactics or blatant manipulation, but for some reason his people always did what he said no matter what. The room was empty while the four gentlemen stood in the pouring rain.

"Gavin, it's been a long time."

He didn't say anything.

"I don't know if you know, or have any idea how hard it's been for me. I try to move on. I do move on! But you're always there. You're never gone, so I'm never truly past you. I want something with you. I want something that doesn't just happen by accident. There's a thing we both have and I think- don't try to argue with this- but I think nobody in the infinite timelines of the universe has ever had what we do."

I was starting to tremble a little bit. There was a brief moment of terror welling up in me right before he responded.

"What do you want me to say? The last time we talked, you didn't seem to feel anything like that. I was actually into you back then. What was it? Six years ago?"

"I was acting, Gavin. Your weird friend was there too and you wouldn't let him leave."

"What?! How the fuck was I supposed to know that? I didn't let Douglass leave, because I thought it would make you uncomfortable to be alone in a room with me!"

"I was uncomfortable. Regardless, are you saying you're not- like- you don't feel-" "Aife, stop. Wait a second. I need to process... I don't know how I feel. You seem like a different person every time we meet. I guess, I've gotten used to you being inconsistent, but-wait- so why am I mad?" he asked genuinely but also rhetorically.

"I think you're mad because I hurt you. I'm sorry. I've never felt like we could last more than a couple nights at most. I hurt you because that's what I wanted. I still want to be with you, arguably a lot more than what is good for my own physical safety. I mean, getting pelted by rocks still hurts no matter how magical you are."

"So... why tonight? And what exactly are you asking me for? Do you just want to fuck or do you want some kind of secret Anikin-Padme marriage situation?"

"I don't know. Like you said, I'm inconsistent. What I do know is that there's never been a point where I didn't care very deeply about you. I just want a little more of you. Maybe somewhere between just fucking and that shitty reference. Are you-"

"I still don't understand what you want, but I think I'm down with it," he said.

Gavin rose from his oversized chair and kissed me. There was no going back from there. It all happened pretty fast- enough so that when the goblins came back inside they didn't seem to suspect anything. It was still very good though. He knows how to get me really on (when he actually tries).

On my walk back home, the rain had stopped. The sky was just as black, but it was warmer now. I was enjoying myself fantasizing about when we scheduled to meet up next when I was hit with a rather concerning thought. Gavin and I engaged in coitous intercouse, and he did not pull out... We rarely did it like that, but when we did, he always had good timing. Was he trying to get me pregnant? This question had a lot of sub-questions that I asked myself for the duration of my trip. Would a child bring us closer together? Could he be a good father? Could I be a good mother? The answer to all three of those particular questions is *no*.

The Problem

After we had several more run-ins that month, I started to sense a parasitic energy in me. It was fetus energy. I was fucking pregnant. I was at a royal feast when this realization fully hit me, so I ran to my room at the top of the palace and cried. I started picturing me and Gavin on a farm with a cute little house and a kid with sheep and a garden, but then I remembered how harmful this visual was for my mental health. So instead, I pictured me getting an abortion and strangling Gavin to death for causing this dreadful inconvenience.

I couldn't get another abortion. It was too much for me the last time. I started mentally sifting through royal couples who I felt were most fit to raise a child. Everyone in my circle was too obsessed with money or themselves to be good parents... except for one couple: Harold and Amy. They were party rockers, but they always talked about calming down at some point. In their early twenties, with good heads on their shoulders, and sincerely kind personalities, it was no competition. I would give them my baby to raise as their own. I still wanted to name him though. I like naming stuff. I think that's one of the few things I'm very good at.

I wasn't in a public relationship at the time, and I didn't want to start one. I had just got a good thing started with Gavin for the first time in a while. It wasn't worth risking. No. I didn't tell him about the baby. Yes. That meant we had to go several months without seeing each other. It also meant I had to self-isolate from pretty much everyone for just as long. I couldn't let people see my belly, and there's no spell to make people look less pregnant.

Shut in and ceasing all in-person communication, everyone assumed I was having a mental breakdown. I was actually just eating a lot and hanging out with Harold and Amy... and having a mental breakdown. I really wanted to see him, and I felt bad knowing he probably wanted to see me too. I wasn't exactly ecstatic about once again negating my maternal instincts in favor of some loose sense of the greater good. I wouldn't say I was being eaten alive, but the guilt was definitely biting.

When little Amergin was born, I gave him to Amy and I knew instantly that she would be a great mother. She looked at him like he was more important than anything. Harold wasn't too far from this vibe. They were awestruck. This was a significant step up from letting a complete stranger adopt my child. I'll carry the guilt of Magic Girl's trauma until the day I die. I knew I could trust those two. It takes a lot of faith to hand your baby to someone and say "it's yours now," but damn. I had the right people to raise him.

The Weird Shit

I found myself too accustomed to the lifestyle of a cow for my own good. After having Amergin and sending my friends off, I decided to stay shut in for a while longer. Plus, I had to think of a dramatic re-appearance. I tried painting, but it was too abstract to look at without retching. Those pictures got repurposed as heating for the throne room. It was a pleasant little life cycle.

I was looking out over central park when I saw Bear. It was strange enough to see him after almost a year, but even more so to see him running through the middle of the park. Mountain people don't run, unless they have a damn good reason. I was too curious to stay inside, so I put on some pants and snuck out.

I've been following Bear through the forest for two days. He's chasing a buggy. He doesn't know I'm on his tail, and I want to keep it that way. Probably four hundred years ago, he confessed his love for me. He just said it once and nothing changed between us. He never went back on it, and I never felt like inquiring. I just didn't want to give him the wrong idea. You know... with me alone following him into the woods. Anyway, that's where I am now. I'm hiding in the woods following a half-senile, old giant with a sword strapped to his back.

Bear is old. He's old even for a mountain person. He's honestly one of my best friends and I don't want him to hurt himself. I also don't want him to hurt someone else. I wouldn't be shocked if he was genuinely invested in some kind of goblin conspiracy at this point. He's been getting a little loopy these past few years. That's me trying to morally justify spying on him. I'm very curious.

King of the Underworld

These are mentally recorded letters written by a time traveling political analyst while under the service of World United sometime in earth's 2440s (I think). The files were snatched by the Shlangovian god, Malkovich. Immediately after, the box-like device on which these records were stored was abruptly reformatted and placed on someone else's head. The letters never reached their destination.

Sunday

Hey mom. I left earth yesterday. Barely over twenty four hours has given me enough time to reevaluate my loyalty to an oath I once made: to never tell anyone about my job. You're dying of cancer while I'm out working. Plus, I think I'm running out of ways to show how much I love you. That's why I'm gonna break my commitment to the government. You've always been so curious about what I do. I don't expect you to go around telling everyone my secrets, and I'll be damned if you die never knowing what I spent most of my waking life doing. Here it is:

I'm a time traveler. I'm also technically a clone of myself. Don't worry. I'm still your daughter with all the same memories. I am just a second body. When they send us to different universes, we can't physically come back. That's why they only send clones to collect intel. That intel is then extracted from our clone brains and shot back into the future- the same future we were sent from. All the knowledge I attain while "out" will be returned to my original body. Any actions taken by me (the clone) are ones that my original body will be held accountable for. I hope that makes sense.

The program I'm in is called the 'Better World Project'. You may have heard of it, but it goes far deeper than anyone would suspect. The branch that employs me (Transuniversal Interview Training) sends me into the last days of inferior worlds where I am to learn what went wrong. Once I've analyzed decades worth of data, I will die. When that happens, my consciousness will be zapped right back into my original body only seconds after I watched myself leave. This is done through a small gray box that stores living memories. Back home, this entire process will only take a matter of minutes. This means that mentally, I'm a lot older than you. That's weird.

I'm presently on my way to a strange, manmade, fucked up alternate reality. I'm floating inside a pitch black orb, bouncing around in the cosmos. I can't see anything and there's nothing to hold on to. It's like how my life feels right now. I don't know. I love you. I'm hoping to see some interesting things when I reach my destination. It's like- fuck it, you know? I'll tell you everything. I think you'll really enjoy it.

Monday

I got here early this morning and walked for miles until I reached the nearest town. There seems to be a lot of kingdoms, but they're all united under one broader empire. Mainly, I'm supposed to interview the most powerful leaders of this planet. I learned that there is one supreme empress of sorts named Aife. I'm going to try and interview her. She's thousands of years old. I'm sure she has a lot of interesting things to say. If it takes me twenty years to get to her, so be it. That's why I'm here.

Then there's the illusive, phantom-like *King of the Underworld*. I'm more interested in him. Like Aife, he's as old as the world. Several natives have informed me that he's a brutal, terrifying demon king who rules the goblins. I have to interview him as well. If I get killed in the process, that's ok. They can always send another clone. It'll just cost them a lot of money.

There are quite a few less significant kings and queens I could speak to, but those two are perfect. Unfortunately, I neglected a sizable portion of the assigned reading on this world, but it is a fact that these particular monarchs were sent here from the future by a mad scientist with a god complex.

I'm staying in a strange little village near the west coast. There are real gnomes here. I've seen aliens before, but this is almost more bizarre than that. Why the hell are they here? And how? They look exactly like the fantasy creatures from earthian Celtic folklore. Upon asking these questions to a friendly bartender, he gave me a stern look and said, "Don't be racist." I didn't press him after that. In truth, I should have done my homework.

Some general observations about this planet: the people here are well-educated on average. There don't seem to be any wars going on, but there is plenty of civil unrest. There are unions, protests, subtly exploitative oil and steel companies, railroads, and several different humanoid people groups. According to that bartender there are humans, mountain people, gnomes, probably trolls, and goblins. To my shock, everyone here speaks english. This planet isn't unashamedly earthian (particularly, British). I have no idea how this all happened, but it's very interesting.

So, I arrived here during the final century of this world. I know from future data, that in seventy years humanity will be stricken by a plague and die out. The other races will be virtually unaffected, but after another twenty years or so the world will be smashed by a comet killing every living thing. There's nothing I can do to stop these things from happening. Even if there was, there's no reason I should try.

After a lengthy conversation with the bartender man, I realized that the empress is untouchable- especially to the public. According to him, she is (and has been for quite some time) isolated in her throne room doing god knows what and allowing no visitors. It feels like everyone is on edge. They don't seem to understand or care when I tell them I'm from the future. Tomorrow I'm taking a train to the capital. It sounds like the ultimate hub of everything (trade, science, entertainment, ect.) I'm gonna do a little studying.

Tuesday

You won't believe this, but wizards are real. They live here. The queen, Aife, is one and there's a legend about an invisible wizard city somewhere in the mountains. I met someone today who claims to be descended from a mighty, legendary wizard named Devin. Allegedly he is eighty two. He doesn't look a day older than twenty five. I interviewed him.

His name was Hevin. Pronounced like heaven. He said he knew a little magic, but the secrets to unlocking one's potential are hidden by the government. In his words, "The only wizards worth having so much power are the ones who wouldn't want to use it." So it appears that lots of people are technically wizards, but they don't know how to tap into their abilities.

We went to a pub in the west end of Bird City. We sat on a wooden balcony and overlooked the Fish River. The "interview" was more like a friendly conversation. Hevin was rough around the edges, but very sweet. After talking with him for quite a while, something stuck out to me about this culture. Not only is it generally progressive, but the people here adore the queen.

I can summarize this popular sentiment in one thing Hevin said. When asked about his feelings on authoritarian versus libertarian rule in Wingland, he looked at me like I was insulting him.

"I don't know what it's like in the future, but you clearly don't know what it's like in the past. We aren't ruled. We are protected. The only rules that exist are there to help everyone thrive. When Queen Aife founded this nation, she ushered in the era of purpose.

Her goal was to alleviate widespread suffering from the planet, so that nobody had to fight for their survival, and everyone could feel a sense of belonging. She helped us reach a point as a society, where anyone could express themselves through art, business, sex, spirituality and so forth. We crossed the threshold of just scraping by. After that, everyone could express themselves without worrying if they were going to eat that day."

"Then, people started to realize that purpose was unattainable. By the year 2,700, Wingland had entered the Age of Absurdism. We knew that the gods exist, but understood that no reaction to their existence would change anything. It became clear that sacrifices didn't matter. As the queen kept telling everyone, 'Reality is your own prerogative, but pain is indisputably bad.' So, people began to live their lives with little regard for rationality unless it directly hurt others. Some kind of abstract philosophy of general nothingness began to emerge. People were cutting their own limbs off as a trend, fashion took a turn for the worst (in my opinion), teenagers were starting moth gangs... yeah it wasn't good."

I asked him what moth gangs were.

"Oh boy. Well you see, the young people would go out and catch hundreds of moths. They put them in baskets, then released them into people's houses. If your house got mothed, you had to join the moth gang or do a silly dance. It sounds innocent, but a lot of people died."

I remembered where we went off track.

"Wait. So, where were you going?" I asked.

"Oh right! Rome! I'm going to Rome and I'm actually late," he said.

"You're going to- you guys have a Rome here?" I asked.

"Well yeah. That's where my girlfriends live."

"Ok ok, but why- wa- does it have like- a caesar?" I asked with a dash of authentic curiosity amidst my chuckling.

"What? No it's just Rome. It has a mayor. I seriously need to go now though. It was great to talk to you!" he said as he got up from his seat. It was golden hour. A soft yellowness blushed over the pine-tree covered landscape. Then I remembered that we had ended on a rabbit trail. I yelled to him while he was making his way through the restaurant.

"Wait! Hang on. What I meant by 'where' was *where* you were going with your answer. We were talking about something to do with the government and culture. I think were trying to make a point?"

"Oh, right!" he said while he approached my table and leaned over a chair. He looked me dead in the eyes.

"Okay. I love Queen Aife. Everyone loves her. She put this whole thing together. She's the undisputed mother of Shlangovia. Without her specifically as the queen, I have no idea how worse everything would be for the world. As for purpose, she at least gives us the chance to look for it. I guess… I don't mind being told what to do by her."

He snatched his bag and sprinted out of the pub. We didn't say goodbye or exchange thank-yous. I couldn't shake the feeling that some of his accounts were exaggerated or otherwise entirely false. Having spoken far too long with one individual, I decided to talk briefly with random people on the street. Most people thought I was insane, but I learned that Hevin was certainly not alone in his sentiments. Everyone generally admired the queen. She single handedly influenced the entirety of this world's infrastructure, cultural shifts, philosophical awakenings, and even architectural feats. She's like if a pop star was president of the world, and a goddess.

I highly doubt that I stand a chance at meeting this genius woman. I'll keep trying though. Another thing: everyone here seems below average intelligence on an earthian scale. They're well educated and have expansive lexicons, but everything they say is a copy of something else. I was reading an article that expressed exactly what Hevin told me almost word for word. It doesn't seem like free thinking is repressed by any means. On the contrary, the government is very keen on encouraging new ideas and fostering openness. Nonetheless, it almost feels like the people don't really utilize independent thought- at least here in the city. I can't tell if they're just brainwashed or if this system has genuinely figured the secret to a prosperous kingdom.

Thursday

Well, yesterday afternoon I was kidnapped. I was walking in a park when a bag went over my head. Within seconds I found myself in a carriage. When they removed the bag it was completely dark. After I had already realized the following I was informed by a soft voice that we were in a cave. Soon that voice's face was illuminated by a lamp. It was a goblin sitting calmly with a joint in his hand. I hadn't seen a goblin before that. There were a lot of emotions happening. According to earthian stereotypes, being kidnapped by a goblin probably means something very bad. Despite my growing fear, I had to admit he looked rather cool.

"Where are we going?" I asked, to my relief, without choking.

"You said you're from the future, you've been harassing people in the streets, your clothes are cool, and you have a weird box on your head, so I'm taking you to the king."

A microsecond of explosive joy was crushed by the idea that I was about to be involved in a Shlangovian goblin scam.

"The king? You don't mean-"

"Yep. I do. King Gavin- Lord of the Underworld. He asked for you personally."

"Oh shit. Oh wow. Ok. Is there anything I should do to prepare? I mean, are we going to see him now?" I asked.

"We've got a three day's journey or so left. He's meeting us halfway."

I didn't even have to try. They're taking me right to him. Granted, this could mean anything. Maybe they'll take me to a village and cook me over a fire. Maybe they really will take to Gavin and he'll have me drawn and quartered on site. Maybe he'll just glance at me and decide that I should be imprisoned for life. It doesn't really matter what he does, I guess. Anyway, I need sleep.

Sunday

I met the King of the Underworld today. It unfolded into one of the most eventful experiences of my life. I was brought into a large, dimly lit, circular room. Opposite of me sat the king on a large throne made of stone. Lining the walls surrounding us had to have been at least fifty guards tightly gripping their weapons. Gavin just stared at me. Nobody was initiating a conversation, so I decided to start my interview. There was a lot of talking, so I'll only include the interesting bits.

So you're the king of the underworld, correct?

"Yes."

Is that job very difficult?

"Emotionally draining."

I can only imagine! Do you feel like your subjects generally regard you with respect?

"Pffft of course. I'm fairly popular."

Aha. How does this place run economically? It seems like you have an entire civilized world down here.

"Well, we don't have physical currency. We exchange favors, goods, services, information, ect. We do have large scale production, but it runs on-"

I'm sorry, did you say you use information as leverage with one another? That smells a like-

"Blackmail."

Yes.

"Too bad I guess. I personally think it works fine."

I gotcha. So, how does law enforcement work down here? I mean what kind of laws do you have?

"Well it's kind of based on the ancient principle of an eye for an eye. Generally everyone stays in line. When they don't, they're penalized by whoever they hurt. You steal a donkey from someone- they can steal an animal from you and something extra. You have to register any time you take a reaction, so people aren't starting feuds. It's simple and sweet. How we've always done it."

That's very interesting! So no police?

"Fuck no. If a problem escalates, it gets brought up to whoever's in charge of that town and it gets taken care of."

Nice... Now, Gavin, I hope this isn't too personal, but the people above seem to really dislike you. It seems like, to humans and gnomes, you're a very bad person. You don't strike me as unkind. Why do you think they feel this way?

"Well, for one, there's been a lot of miscommunication through the ages. Actually, that's about the extent of the problem."

How so?

"Ok so, when I was cursed, the whole thing was that I would be hated by mankind and never die. The gods only cursed me because they thought I was lying about something. I wasn't lying. They were just confused. Then, one time, one of the southern goblin clans raided a city and killed almost everyone in it. I think the city was called Drain or something. Anyway, it was a very racist town, and a kid got beaten to death by some knights. A little game of telephone ensued through the chain of command concerning how to handle this. It went back and forth between the chief of that clan and I. Somewhere down the line, somebody misinterpreted my orders which were 'Don't do a thing,' to quote myself exactly. Filtered through several generals, and a handful of horseback messengers, somehow it turned into 'Kill everyone inside.' I know. Someone was being a little rat. I never found out who. Anyway, everyone thinks I'm a bloodthirsty murderer because of that. I've personally thrown out a few bad eggs, but only out of pure necessity. I never let my people go around killing. That's not cool."

That's very unfortunate. I'm sorry. What about espionage? I was told that you have spies watching the world; that they even go around meddling in the affairs of inventors, artists, scientists, ect.

"I'm not gonna talk about any of that."

Alrighty. So it seems to me like you're very misunderstood. Do you ever think about clearing your name?

"I've thought about it, but- well- I don't know. It's just not a good idea."

Why not?

"I highly doubt someone your age would understand."

I'm fifty three.

"Sorry. You look a little younger than that. I'm like- almost three thousand. My statement still applies. You're like a little baby to me. No offense."

None taken, sweety.

"Is Elijah still alive?"

Oh dear. He sure is.

"How's he doing?"

He's several miles underground in a top secret prison somewhere.

"Good for him. What year is it where you're from?"

Very very far into the future. I don't mean to cut you off, but I'm hoping to keep this dialogue more centered around you if that's ok. Let me know if these questions become intrusive, but how do you feel about your placement in the cosmos?

"How I feel is pretty much irrelevant, but ok. Let's get existential then! There's a lot of moral ambiguity with what Elijah was doing. On one hand, he helped people find beautiful lives that they never would have had the chance to otherwise. On the other, that's arguably a very questionable use of power. It causes a lot of problems. That's not to mention the instances where he intentionally gave people bad lives. Honestly, I love what I do. I like this place even more than earth, but I would never have chosen it if I knew all the bad shit that was ahead, you know? He played the judge, jury and executioner in a way. I hate that. I think it's kind of terrible."

I feel that. It's a good thing he's not hurting anyone anymore, huh?

This is where Gavin started crying. He leaned far back in his oversized throne and covered his face. At this point in the interview, I honestly gave up. I just wanted to get to know this guy. I just wasn't feeling all the diplomatic shit. Keep in mind, this can get me fired.

My name is Francis. You seem to have had a painful life.

"Oh it's been a crazy time alright... I get by. Would you like to know what we do for fun here?"

Why not.

"Ok cool. So, we have a lot of sports, but my favorite is the couple fights."

Dear god.

"So basically, couples kinda get to hash out their issues in a big metal cage. They just beat the shit out of each other until one of them gives up."

That sounds awful, Gavin.

"It's wonderful. It gives them a chance to let out their energy. Last week, a guy kicked his boyfriend's jaw and broke it. It was fucking awesome. I think you should come see a match sometime."

I'm good. It seems like you're culture is very barbaric.

"That's one way to put it. I prefer the term 'fun.' I bet you'd have some if you came to see couple fighting."

No.

"Ok. You're obviously very boring. Give me another boring question then. Go on."

Have you had many lovers?

"Woah! Okay then. I mean, not really? I've had affairs with a queen or two- several flings, but I haven't been able to fully invest in someone. It's actually kind of complic- hey guys? Can you all leave? I need to have some privacy for this conversation."

All the goblins vacated but one.

Who's he?

"That's Mr. Douglas the three hundred and thirty first."

That's a lot of Douglases. You know Gavin, he was rather hospitable- putting a bag over my head and carrying me away. Such a gentleman.

"He's one in a long, sacred line of assistants. Every Douglas I've ever had has been my best friend. Mr. Douglas, say something!"

Douglas stared into my eyes and calmly uttered, "Cunt." Gavin burst into hysterical laughter.

"Douglas! You cheeky bastard!"

Ok, but Gavin... why did you empty the room?

"I just wanna vent, ma'am if that's ok. You're nice and you're from another universe. You probably don't care about using this against me. Mr. Douglas is the only person who knows, but I haven't been able to talk to another human about it."

About what?

"Aife."

What about her?

"Well, I've fallen in love with her a few times. Right now is one of those times."

Gavin's voice was getting a little shaky. His cheeks were red. I was witnessing something truly sad unfold.

Oh my god. The queen of the world? You're- oh- oh wow. I'm sorry.

"It's ok, Francis. I mean... no. It's really fucking not."

I guess that puts you in a rather strange position.

"MMMM... You think?" he growled while he gripped his arm rests- clearly trying to eschew the flow of tears.

You can tell me anything, Gavin. I won't rat.

"Do you even care to know?"

We don't know each other, but I have a feel for where you are. I know what it's like to live in an abyss.

"Fuck! Fuck. Please don't call it that. Damnit. Alright... You're good. I'm sorry."

He took a few deep breaths.

"As far as the public is concerned, we are arch enemies. She's this pure, virgin Mary archetypal figure. I'm like a demon. We agreed to keep it that way. We've always disagreed on the fundamentals of ruling the world, and our people generally dislike each other. We are kind of enemies- but like, enemies who can't fight because they both have too much leverage- and that have fucked each other a few times."

I spat out my water. This viscerality was the first thing to make Douglas crack a smile.

I'm sorry WHAT?

"Hehe yeah. We used to meet sometimes in secret just to talk about stuff, but we went through some phases where things got pretty complicated. She would get feelings for me, then I would feel bad for her, but I still had enough resentment to not be in love with her at that moment, because it took her so long to finally be in love with me. Then we'd fuck and one of us would always feel like shit. We just go through these crazy cycles. It's been ripping me apart for thousands of years."

Holy shit.

"That's right. And I still don't know where we're at."

Have you asked her recently how she feels?

"Uh... I think everyone in Wingland knows how she feels. She's been having a breakdown for several months now- locked herself in- ghosted everyone. I don't know if you've heard about all that. She won't respond to my letters and I can't just sneak into her place. I worry about her now. I've barely ever had to do that."

So you and her would have secret meetups and then she just stopped showing up?

"Yeah man. She ghosted me. Not too long ago, we were meeting like every other week or so. Then with no warning whatsoever, she cut off all contact."

Damn.

"I can't physically sleep. When I stop to think about her I usually start shaking uncontrollably. I've had not one- not two- but twelve seizures. This is the worst part of being immortal. You just can't fucking-"

Then BOOM. A cave wall burst open. A huge metal gauntlet emerged. Amidst the rubble and dust towered a giant man. He was probably close to eight feet tall and extremely muscular. He was clad in armor with a sheath on his back. A gray beard reached all the way to his belt buckle. Nobody said a word. A mountain person had just punched open the wall, and he didn't look happy. He broke the silence with a roaring monologue.

"GAVIN! Lord of the Underworld, Father of Darkness- I am King Bear, son of King Turtle, son of Dog! My grandfather watched you murder his best friend, Fart, with his own eyes. Then, with my own eyes, I saw piles of my people burning in the streets. They were all slain the night before by your very soldiers. You have been the enemy of every good creature under the sun since the beginning of time. No longer will you plague the mind of our sweet queen! Your day of atonement has arrived. The second ancient prophecy of Apple will now come to fruition! With my own-"

"Wait- which one is that?" Gavin interjected. King Bear ignored him.

"I'm not just gonna kill you, Gavin. I'm gonna cut out your eyes. I'm gonna peel the skin off your face. I'm gonna castrate you. I'm going to do everything to you that goblins have done to people, and much more!" said the giant with a twisted smile.

"Gavin could kill you just by looking at you. He also can't die you fucking moron," stated Douglas.

"Not usually! But as the prophecy foretold, there is one way. There is one blade that can quench the flame of Gavin's soul."

"How'd you find us by the way?" asked Gavin.

"I followed your carriage. Please let me speak." With that, Bear unsheathed a very large sword.

"Hey! That's my old sword! Where the hell did you get that?" Gavin yelled.

Bear just held it up and recited a prophecy.

"The bleeding heart of a dying land
Will find its way to a hero's hands.
One day when all is growing dim,
What the devil once held will return to him.
His breath will stop, for among the rocks
Is hiding what he needs.
He hides so far within the clock,
But one day while he bleeds
He'll finally know the brutal toll
Of delaying destiny!"

"Uh Bear... I don't think that means what you-"

Before Gavin could finish his sentence, his bowels had been spilled on the floor. Soon his arms and legs were amputated. By the time his eyes were gouged out, hundreds of goblins entered the room and swarmed the giant; slashing him with all kinds of weapons. Guts and limbs were flung around. I just hid in the corner watching. This wasn't the first time a blood bath had gone down right in front of me, but I'd never been in a situation like this one.

Gavin and Bear were now completely buried under a small army. The huge sword was swiping through the swarm- killing handfuls at a time. I lit a joint, closed my eyes, and tried to dissociate. Then, a yellow light erupted into the hall of stone illuminating everything.

There was Aife glowing. She was sprinting towards the death pile. She dove right into the center of it. In seconds, the flailing stopped. The goblins moved back and dispersed. The three monarchs were sprawled on the ground covered in blood. Aife was no longer glowing. Her left arm was gone and she had been impaled. Gavin was scattered around the room. Bear's chest had a burnt hole in it and he was coughing.

"Aife! Why?" he cried out.

"Bear, this wasn't supposed to happen."

"But the prophecy!"

"What prophecy?" Aife yelled.

"The one from Apple. She said- AGh. What the fuck, Aife! Why did you try to stop me?" "Look at this. Look at them!" she gestured to the dead and wounded goblins now outnumbering the unharmed ones.

"Aife, I killed him. I stopped him. Society can finally move past him! Why- why are you even here?" Bear asked. He started coughing up blood. Aife took a long moment to examine her surroundings. She sat up and her arm started to grow back. With a sigh she began.

"Bear, I didn't want anyone to get hurt..."

"Aife, I love you." he said. Upon hearing this she was instantly in tears.

"I love you too, Bear- and thank you for everything you've done. Your name will always be remembered in history. Sleep peacefully now. You've avenged your people."

The giant smiled. With a few whispered words (I couldn't decipher) he drifted away. Aife abruptly stopped crying. I think she was faking it for him.

During that final conversation, the goblins had already started locating Gavin's various severed body parts and putting them in a pile. It seemed like this wasn't their first time doing it. When Aife noticed me sitting in the corner, she remained equally as dead pan. She saw the machine attached to my head and stepped over several bodies to get to me.

"So you're from the future?" she asked.

"I- yes." This woman stood a head higher than me. Given what I had just seen, you would think that should be her least intimidating feature.

"Gavin isn't dead. That sword's not magical at all. It's just big with words on it," she said quite matter-a-factly.

"Bear probably mistook one of my old love poems for a vengeful prophecy or something. I'm surprised he found that sword though. Were you wanting to interview me?"

"Um. If that's ok?" I said.

"Only if you let me hit that," she said and gestured to my joint.

I rolled her another one. We awkwardly watched the goblins clean up bodies while we smoked. It was eerie, but kind of nice. I wondered if maybe she was the single coolest person I'd ever met. I realized where Gavin was coming from in terms of his unruly attraction.

Monday

When Gavin reconstructed and healed, him and Aife reunited. He wanted to know why she disappeared for so long. She said it was because she was having a prolonged manic depressive episode. That's what everyone assumed it was anyway. Despite Gavin being very upset with her, they still made out right in front of me. It was like I wasn't even there. It was kind of cute and disgusting.

I'm sure this is all beyond shocking to you. I was pretty surprised by it all myself. So, now you know what I do. This will be the last letter I write to you. This is probably the most interesting it's gonna get here. Honestly, the only reason I'm still wearing the box is so that I can print these letters out when I get back. I'll have to be very clever about getting them past the data scanner somehow. It probably won't work if I'm being realistic. If that's the case, I'll just relay the key elements to you in person. Anyway, I love you! I can't wait to see you again.

Francis

The End of the World

I have never been in a romantic relationship. I've been searching for someone my whole life. It's not like I don't know what love is. I was in it once or twice. Both times it was of the unrequited type. I've known many people to fancy me, but nobody ever seemed right for me. Now that I'm sitting here watching flames from heaven fall into the ocean, I'm starting to wonder if I should have settled. Recently, I decided it would be interesting to document the end of the world. I like the idea of being the last person ever to write something down.

I wasn't raised by my real parents. When I was a baby, my mother gave me away to her friends. Those friends are who I knew to be my parents for the first thirty years of my life or so. Their names were Harold and Amy. I grew up in a very tense household. Harold and Amy had some of the most toxic relationship dynamics I've ever seen. I was their only adopted child, but they treasured me above their own two biological offspring, Nathan and Beth. I don't want to talk about all the terrible shit that unfolded in that family. All that's important is that I left them when I was thirty.

Eventually, my mother cracked and told me who my real parents were. I had known I was adopted my whole life, but I always assumed my real parents were deceased. As it turned out, they were both alive and well. I wasn't too upset with them, but I was curious enough to break into my mom's house.

My mother is Aife. My father is Gavin. This explained everything. I didn't even have to ask them questions. I just knew what happened. As it goes with royalty, public appearances are more pressing than the sanctity of mental health. Aife looked up at me terrified. She seemed unfamiliar with the sight of a man with giant black bird wings. My eyes were also fully black. She was slumping back in her throne as if to admit defeat. Hunched over her was more than likely the most powerful wizard to ever exist (me). Seeing her terror, my intimidating form dissolved. We didn't speak a word, but I think she knew exactly what was happening. It wasn't part of my plan to let her live, or to start crying, but I did both of those things while she gave me a big hug.

She told me about my dad. He didn't even know about me. I wanted him to. From what Aife said, he sounded like a very cool guy. I would have never guessed that the King of the Underworld himself was my dad. Although, it does make perfect sense. I took a more docile approach to meeting him. I signed a plethora of documents which took weeks to be processed and approved. No less than a month after trying to get an appointment with his secretary, there I was walking down into a deep cave. My meeting with the gatekeeper went smoothly until he found out that I was a wizard. At which point he promptly exited the office leaving papers flying through the air. He was panting upon re-entrance, clearly having run quite a distance.

"King Gavin would like to speak with you as soon as possible, sir," he said as professionally as possible between gasping breaths.

I was led down yet another massive stone corridor in Gavin's cave home. A few lamps lining the walls fostered a dimly lit, dungeon-like atmosphere. We walked for a very long time. My hypnotic state was interrupted by the sight of the man himself- Gavin. He stood in the middle of the hall trying to catch his breath. Upon seeing my face, he was beaming. He knew instantly who I was. We bore an uncanny resemblance. Laughing, he came sprinting forth and tackled me to the ground. It was the most odd experience of my life.

As one would expect, this turn of events caused a bit of a rift between my parents. Aife withholding the knowledge of my existence from Gavin could well be regarded as a bad move. Understandably, Gavin threw a tumultuous tantrum... in front of me... and Aife... and some lady named Francis. He snatched Aife's crown off her head and did just about everything physically imaginable to utterly obliterate it. She had no outward response to this. Neither did Francis or I.

"Gavin, I'm sorry," Aife eventually said while Gavin was pacing around the room. We were meeting in a dungeon beneath the city.

"You have some of the biggest fucking balls I've ever seen, my beautiful queen" "I didn't want to hurt you. I don't want to hurt anyone. Everything I do is-" Gavin proceeded to mock her in a rather undignified manner.

"'*I didn't want to hurt you*' Shut the fuck up! He's my damn son! Shut up! Look at him!" He pointed at me and I tried to avoid the trajectory of his finger. This was irrational of me, but I was very uncomfortable and I didn't know what to do.

"You just never thought to yourself, 'oh maybe Gavin would at least want to know about his FUCKING SON!' Oh my god! You insufferable bitch! Why the fuck am I still in love with you?" Gavin's rage was out of control at this point. He very clearly wished he had raised me himself.

"And the fact that you- you thought HAROLD of all people would be a better father. I've never doubted your judgement of character, but you clearly didn't know that man."

"Gavin, he and Amy were two of my closest friends. He seemed gentle and kind." "Yeah! So gentle. His first move was to exploit his son's power to conquer a kingdom!

Why do- no. I know why, but it's so stupid! It's stupid. There's no way this isn't just you being selfish."

I believe that he crossed the line there. The stream of insults slid right off her, but that final comment broke the floodgates. She didn't reply verbally, but her crying was loud enough to say something to Gavin.

"Gavin, you need to take all of that back right now," Francis said.

"No he doesn't. He's- he hit the mark. He's on to something I think," Aife sputtered. I walked over to her and put my hand on her back. What the hell else was I supposed to do?

"FUCK. Fuck. No- no it's not true, Aife. Nothing that I just said was true. Damnit. I'm just mad. I know how much you care. I should've just not spoken." This was the fastest I'd ever seen a man apologize.

"I need a blunt. I'll talk to you all later." And there she went.

That night, the four of us had dinner along with Saorsie and her girlfriend. It was surprisingly light hearted for the conversation that transpired not more than two hours before. We drank a lot of wine. Gavin and Saorsie played several beautiful songs while everyone else danced. I got a big lump in my throat, because in all honesty, I had never experienced a positive family gathering in my life. Something about the way my parents acted around each other was intoxicating. Their fights were dramatic and terrifying, but I soon learned that this was their version of flirting. They seem to get excited by it. When they talk, it's like they share one brain. It was difficult to take in. After thousands of years they were still in love, dancing around with their friends. They are by far the most intriguing couple I've ever encountered.

So, if I recall correctly, it was about this time that the great plague was sweeping the world. Humans in particular were dying at a concerning rate. This disease killed you the week you found out you had it. Back then, if you lived in the country and rarely went to town, you were probably fine, but eventually it hit everyone. That's why Gavin, Aife, Saorsie, her girlfriend, Francis, and I fled to Wizard City in the north. I was told my whole life that this place was a lie. To my shock, it was a real place full of magical people who were immune to the plague. It was hidden in a mountain valley high above the clouds and guarded by trolls. I didn't know those were real either.

It was hopeless for everyone. The disease would manifest anytime it was combated, so eventually it would go to wipe out all humans, gnomes, and goblins. It was only at the last stages of hope that Aife realized there was nothing she could do. Everyone was left to fend for themselves. This nightmare is what brings me here.

I am writing this for myself only. I want to think about all these things before I die. According to Francis (who died a while back), the world is going to end on this very day. My parents believe her. They also believe that their fate is tied to that of the planet's. Francis claimed that once fire rained down on Shlangovia and sank the continent, Gavin and Aife would finally perish.

Everyone is kind of doing their own thing right now. A lot of wizards are getting drunk or having sex. My parents and I decided to sit on a cliff overlooking the ocean. The sun was just beginning to set right as the fireballs came hurtling through the atmosphere. It's kind of nice to die at the same time as them. It feels kind of beautiful. I've done a lot of really bad shit, and so have they, but nothing matters now. Aife rests her head on Gavin's shoulder and I hear them briefly converse.

"It's kind of weird how long it took for us to- just be together" Gavin says.

"Was it worth it?" she asks him.

"Maybe. Probably not, but I am happy."

"Me too."

"Angela, I love you."

"Well, I love you too, Gavin."

I don't deserve to witness this moment. It doesn't deserve to be reduced to ink on paper.

I had never seen love like this. My adopted parents hated each other.

They keep whispering. They turn to look at me sitting by myself behind them. They ask me to come sit with them under their blanket. I do so. The three of us silently watch the sky fall over the sea. A wave of apocalyptic proportions is seen far off in the distance. The last words I ever hear are "We love you, Amergin." The tidal wave is here. In its vastness I see the perfect conclusion to my story. From its foaming mouth, I hear the final chord of the world's song strike with a roaring ferocity. It's the end.

Epilogue

Given these stories are all true, I should note that there is a lot more that I could include. I won't, however. I want to maintain the simplicity of it. There's not much to say in conclusion. I think everything speaks for itself. To top off the book I'll include one last poem.

Mountains, Flowers, Night.
Opening, fighting, closing.
Rocks, bees, water.

In death is love.
In love is death.
You're somewhere in the middle.

Reach into my river,
You eternal bitch.
Fuck me until I die.